JENNY'S SONG

JENNY'S SONG

VeraLee Wiggins

REVIEW AND HERALD® PUBLISHING ASSOCIATION
WASHINGTON, DC 20039-0555
HAGERSTOWN, MD 21740

This book was
Edited by Raymond H. Woolsey
Designed by Bill Kirstein
Cover illustration by Mitchell Heinze

PRINTED IN U.S.A.

R&H Cataloging Service

Wiggins, Veralee, 1928-
    Jenny's song.

    I. Title.

ISBN 0-8280-0493-5

Dedication

To my best helper, my most ardent
fan, my most faithful supporter, my love—my everything.

1

A roar shook the apartment building. Jenny Cornell rushed to the kitchen window to see the cause of it. She sucked in a short breath as a huge motorcycle skidded sideways in the street, nearly tipped over, righted itself, and thundered onto the back lawn. Jenny didn't know anyone who drove one of those things, and the face protector concealed the rider's identity. Frightened, she hoped the cyclist, whoever he was, would turn around and leave without causing any trouble.

As she watched furtively from behind the curtain, Jenny wished her new roommate were on hand to help meet this threat.

Roommate! That thought brought another cloud to Jenny's mind. Charlene Haywood would not only be her new roommate but also her new aide in the third-grade room at McKay Creek School. No doubt Charlene was a nice girl, but she seemed so—wild. Bushy red hair, too much makeup, and that voice! Jenny shuddered, remembering Charlene's loud voice. So different from her own quiet ways.

Movement on the lawn brought Jenny back to her immediate problem. Where was Charlene, anyway? She should have been here by now. Somehow she had a feeling that nothing ever scared that girl. The cyclist strode toward the back door.

Should I open it or lock it? Jenny wondered as she hurried to the door. Her heart beat hard against her chest. Then, through the door glass she saw the biker jerk off "his" helmet—it was Charlene, shaking out her red hair. Jenny felt herself sag with relief. After several deep breaths she dashed outside, speechless, and pointed to the cycle.

"Yeah," Charlene said, laughing loudly. "Isn't it neat?"

"But—but—where are your things?" Jenny asked after a long moment.

Charlene pointed to the luggage carrier over the back wheel, filled to capacity with a large dilapidated cardboard box. "There it is. All my worldly possessions." She unstrapped the box and started to the house, cradling it in her arms.

"Whoa! Is this a palace or what?" Charlene asked, when she saw the deep carpet, richly painted rooms, and wraparound glass wall overlooking Pendleton, Oregon.

Jenny led the way to the second bedroom and Charlene dumped the dusty box on the ruffled yellow bedspread. Jenny winced. Well, this was going to be the girl's room so she could treat it as she pleased. "You have your own matching bathroom, Charlene," she said, nodding toward a half-open door. "Would you like to eat before you unpack?"

After supper Jenny cleaned up the kitchen, then relaxed in the living room, reading the paper, while Charlene settled into her bedroom. It would probably be nice having someone in the house with her. But she would have preferred to be alone.

If she could have been satisfied to drive her old clunker for her first year of teaching, and had found a cheaper place to live, she wouldn't have ended up in this financial mess. Oh, well, maybe this arrangement would work out. Jenny relaxed and her head nodded.

A sound like a bull moose with a toothache jerked Jenny not only awake but to her feet. She teetered dangerously, then realized the sound came from Charlene's room.

Running to the room, Jenny jerked open the door and saw her new roommate gyrating wildly around, arms over her head, and snapping her fingers. Jenny put her hands over her ears and stepped into the room; she quickly changed her mind and ran out, slamming the door.

She turned on the TV and sat down. Charlene's stereo drowned out the TV sound so she turned it louder. Still unable to hear, she flipped the thing off and ran out of the house. She could get the milk now as well as later.

When Jenny returned, she hesitated on the kitchen steps and listened. Silence. Golden silence. She opened the door and stepped inside. The TV was going, but quietly. Jenny put away the milk and breakfast cereal, then hurried into the living room.

"Hi, Miss Cornell," Charlene shouted, and returned her attention to the program.

Jenny sat in the rocker and rested her stockinged feet on the coffee table. Turning her eyes to the TV, she saw a man creeping along a window ledge with a drawn gun. He peered into the lighted window a moment, then brought the butt of his gun against the pane. As the glass crashed, the camera panned to the street below, where the cars looked like insects with lights. Then it cut to a commercial.

Jenny drew in a long shuddering breath. "What an awful program."

Charlene leaned back on the couch. Her green eyes sparkled. "Yeah, isn't it delicious, Miss Cornell?" she yelled.

Miss Cornell. Jenny sighed. After school today she had asked Charlene to call her Jenny. "Charlene," she began, unmindful that the program would return any moment, "do I seem old to you?"

Charlene surprised Jenny by taking a moment to think about it. She cocked her head and squinted her eyes. Finally she shook her head. "Not really, Miss Cornell."

Not really? The girl had to stop and decide whether 23 was old? She couldn't be *that* much older than Charlene. Jenny sighed again, more audibly this time. "Why don't you call me Jenny then? That Miss Cornell stuff makes me feel like an old maid."

Charlene gasped. "OK, Miss—I mean, Jenny. I didn't mean . . ." Her voice drifted into silence when the program resumed.

As the story continued, Jenny commented on violent programming and its effect on society.

Finally, unable to watch any longer, she snatched her library book and went to bed. Several chapters later a tiny tap at her bedroom door brought her back to reality. "Come in," she called, grabbing a tissue and stuffing it into the book to mark her place.

Charlene opened the door and peeked around it. "Miss Cor—Jenny, are you awake?" She spoke softly, the first time Jenny had heard Charlene's voice at less than 100 decibels.

"Sure, come in," Jenny answered.

Charlene crept in on tiptoe as though she wouldn't wake Jenny for the world. "Is everything all right?" she whispered.

"Would you like to talk?" Jenny whispered back. Then she giggled. "Why are we whispering?" she asked, trying to speak in a normal voice. She motioned to a padded brass chair by the vanity. "Bring the chair over and sit down."

Charlene obeyed, turned her large eyes on Jenny and said nothing.

"How old are you, Charlene?" Jenny asked kindly.

Charlene licked her lips. "Twenty." She peered at Jenny with a quizzical look in her eyes. "I went to Blue Mountain Community College last winter. I have my aide certificate."

Jenny smiled. "Don't worry about school, you're a good aide."

Charlene leaned toward Jenny, resting her elbows on the bed. "Why do I think things didn't go well tonight?" she asked.

Jenny smoothed the sheet where it folded over the pink quilt. "Maybe because I wasn't too nice. You see, I have nightmares if I watch even the teeniest bit of violence. But I love to read in bed so I guess we don't have a problem there."

Charlene relaxed. "Good. I really like it here and want it to work. Just tell me if I do anything you don't like."

"Just one more little thing. Tonight your music was so loud I couldn't hear the TV."

Charlene's eyebrows shot up. "I'm sorry, Mi—Jenny. I'll keep it down after this. Don't you like rock?"

Jenny laughed, embarrassed. "Not especially. You see, I started piano and voice lessons when I was 6 and learned only classical music. But that wasn't rock you had going, was it?"

Charlene nodded. "Yeah, heavy metal." After a moment she continued, "You wouldn't believe it, but I never listened to anything but religious music at home, and we didn't even have TV."

"I see," Jenny said. "Well, I'll keep my classical music down, too. I'll bet you don't like that. By the way, do I do anything you don't like?"

Charlene sat up straight and nodded, her eyes twinkling. "Yeah. Could you possibly call me Charley?"

"No problem, Charley," Jenny said, laughing. "That name fits you better, anyway."

The next night Jenny barely had the TV turned on when the racket Charley called music rattled the house again. *I can't leave every night,* Jenny thought as she headed for Charley's bedroom. Opening the door with such force it slammed against the wall, she burst inside.

"Charley!" she yelled. Charley, face pointed at the stars and fingers snapping over her head, heard only the music.

Jenny walked over and grasped Charley's shoulders. Charley jerked to a standstill and raised her bushy eyebrows. Jenny pointed to the little stereo. "Turn it down," she shouted.

"What?" Charley screamed, making no move to lower the volume.

Jenny marched over and jabbed the button, turning the machine off. Charley's face reddened and the muscles in her neck tightened. "Why'd you do that?" she yelled. "I'm gettin' my exercise."

"Go for a walk," Jenny said, a smile lifting the corners of her mouth.

Charley didn't return the smile. "Old people like you walk," she snapped. She walked to the dresser and pulled several bills from under her socks. "Here's my first month's rent." She tossed them at Jenny and turned on the stereo.

Jenny punched the music off once more. "This isn't a matter of money, Charley," she said softly, "but of sanity. We have to figure a way to live together." She shrugged. "Or we can't. It's as simple as that."

"You're kidding." Charley looked unconvinced. "You really can't handle this music?"

Jenny shook her dark head slowly. "I really can't, Charley. Sorry."

Charley thought a moment. Then a coarse laugh rumbled from her chest. She flipped on the stereo and turned down the volume. "Is that better?"

"That's great," Jenny said happily. "Now you be sure to tell me if I do something you can't handle."

Charley looked at Jenny a long moment with an unreadable expression. "You're OK, Jenny. I wish I were perfect like you." She turned away and began dancing again.

Jenny wandered back to the living room, wondering if Charley had been sarcastic about that "perfect" stuff. She watched the Jeopardy program, thankful for the quiet.

The girls co-existed peacefully for the next few days, learning to know and enjoy each other. Early Sunday morning they cleaned the apartment and washed the Mustang, then sat on the kitchen steps drinking sodas. Charley looked at the little red car gleaming in the sunshine. "Ever loaned out your car?" she yelled.

Jenny felt a rock land in her stomach. Her pride and joy? The little jewel that ate so much of her paycheck each month? She gulped. "Not yet," she answered in a small voice.

Charley took a swallow of Seven-Up and smiled into Jenny's blue eyes. "Just wondered." She drained her can and stood up. "Guess I'll take a shower."

Jenny followed her into the house, feeling guilty about the car. But why should she? It was hers and it took a lot of sacrifice to own it.

Later, as the girls read the Sunday paper, Jenny kept thinking she should apologize for not lending her car. She folded the comic section and laid it down. "Charley, do you think your cycle's dangerous?"

Charley's green eyes grinned over the paper. "Whoa!" she roared. "That cycle's safe as sittin' on your couch."

"Why did you want to borrow the car then?" Jenny asked, feeling relieved.

Charley dumped her paper on the floor. "Ward and I wanted to go for a last picnic before winter. That's all."

"Can't you go on the cycle?"

"Yeah, but we wanted to go up in the mountains and it's gettin' pretty cool up there."

Jenny unfolded the comics and tried to read Garfield but couldn't concentrate. "When were you thinking about going?" she asked.

Charley glanced out the window at the warm sunshine and shrugged. "Well, we hoped to go today, but it didn't work out."

Jenny's conscience stabbed her. She didn't need her car until late afternoon. She tried to continue reading but still couldn't concentrate. She sneaked another peak at Charley. "How far is the trip you had planned?" she asked, hoping Charley would tell her to forget it.

Charley's blue-lidded eyes captured Jenny's. She leaned back and clasped her hands behind her head, her lips moving as though silently figuring. "Oh, 150 miles, I guess," she answered.

"When could you be back?"

Charley jumped up, jerked Jenny to her feet and hugged her thoroughly. "Thanks," she bellowed into Jenny's ear. "Thanks a lot. We'll be back anytime you say."

"I have a little trip planned this evening," Jenny said, "to my folks' place, in LaGrande, for supper, so I'll need the car by four o'clock."

"No problem." Charley dashed to the phone.

An hour later Jenny leaned into the car as Charley's boyfriend, Ward, eased down the driveway. "The car isn't broken in yet, so please don't go over 55," she said, pulling her head from the moving vehicle.

Ward gave her the thumbs-up sign. "Don't worry, I'll take care of her like she was my own."

"That's what I'm afraid of," Jenny mumbled to herself as she walked back to the house.

When the cuckoo finally struck three o'clock, Jenny hit the shower, glad the lonely day had ended. She put on a black pleated skirt, silky white blouse with a fluffy red bow, and carefully applied enough make-up to look decent.

She stacked all the newspapers and straightened the apartment. She checked the clock—3:45. She walked to the window and watched for the Mustang. And watched and watched. She checked the clock again—3:47.

After another eon the hands pointed to 3:50. She turned on the TV, determined she wouldn't look at the clock again until Charley walked through the door. She watched TV until she realized she didn't know what the program was about, and peeked at the clock—4:05. She switched the TV off. Somehow she'd had a hunch those kids would prove irresponsible. Why had she let her rotten conscience goad her into this, anyway?

At six o'clock she called her folks and canceled out. At nine o'clock she put on her robe and sat stiffly on the couch, too upset to read or even watch TV.

At midnight she called the police, who refused to take the delayed return seriously. At that point Jenny didn't know whether to be positively furious or worried. They could have been in an accident—or—what did she really know about Charley? They could could be in another state by now.

2

Jenny awakened with a start to see Charley leaning over her. Realizing that Charley and Ward were all right, anger welled up in Jenny. She looked from one to the other, then at the clock. Three o'clock!

"I suppose you have a fantastic excuse for ruining my evening as well as scaring me to death," she said quietly, determined to remain calm.

"Yes," Charley said in a voice that probably awakened everyone on the block, "as a matter of fact, we do. Your dumb car broke down."

"My car? My new car?" *Could it have?* Jenny thought. *No way.* She met Charley's gaze. "Where's the car now?"

Ward nodded toward the garage. "Right out there."

"Who fixed it and what was wrong?" Jenny asked.

"Nobody fixed it," Ward said. "It just died while we drove in the mountains. We tried everything we could think of. Finally the engine wouldn't even turn over until an old woman in a big Chrysler stopped and jump-started us. You better have it checked out."

After breakfast the next morning the girls dumped their dishes into the sink. "I suppose you're sticking to your story," Jenny said. "You wouldn't put me to the effort of taking the car to the shop just to keep out of trouble, would you?"

Charley shook her red mop. "That thing wouldn't run for anything. I'm driving my bike so I'll be sure to get home."

The car ran fine and Jenny wondered about Charley's story. But after school she took it back to Pendleton Ford and waited in a small line at the service window.

When she stepped up to the window, the service manager had his back to her, putting something into a file drawer. He turned around. "Now, may I . . . ?" Their eyes met and locked. Jenny had never seen such soft brown eyes. Her breath left in a soft "whish."

After an eternity he jerked his eyes from hers and looked down at a paper he held, studying it as though it held life or death interest to him. A moment later he took a deep breath and met her eyes again. "May I help you?" he asked pleasantly.

As she told him what had happened to the car she drank in his clean good looks. His full-cut dark brown hair feathered softly back except the bit that fell over his forehead. His straight nose looked positively patrician on his clean-shaven face. She gathered herself together. "Do you think it's all right now?" she asked.

He shook his head. "Machines don't heal up. Could he have flooded it?"

Jenny shrugged. "I don't know. He's just a kid."

He smiled and deep dimples appeared in his square face. Jenny put her hands on the desk to steady herself.

"Could you leave the car now or would you rather bring it back in the morning?" he asked.

She couldn't think. She had trouble breathing. "Well," she finally squeaked, several notes higher than her normal voice. She tried again. "I don't have another car and I work." There, at least it was a semblance of her own voice.

"We're closing up here in five minutes," he said, after a moment's silence. "I'll drive you home. Will you be able to find a way to work tomorrow?" He looked as though he really cared.

"I guess I can take the bus," she said. "This is a lot of trouble if those kids made up the whole thing."

Jenny tried desperately to think of something to talk about on the drive to her apartment, but her mouth felt as though it were full of raw oatmeal and her brain took a long vacation. Eventually they arrived at her place.

He waved and smiled that unbelievable smile again. "We'll try to have your car ready by early afternoon."

Jenny stood on the street until the car disappeared, then ran into the apartment. Charley, busy doing something in the kitchen, paused. "Did you get it fixed?" she asked.

Jenny plopped down at the table and took several deep breaths before she answered. "No, it was too late." She put her hand on Charley's arm. "Charley, you won't believe the service manager. He's the most fantastic guy I ever saw." She described him, finishing with "I really can't explain it, but he's an angel and All American Boy rolled into one."

Charley's eyes rolled back into her head. "I gotta see this," she said. "He sounds even better than Ward."

"Ward? He's not even in the running." After a bit more bantering Jenny asked, "Why don't you go with me to pick up the car tomorrow?"

"You couldn't keep me away," Charlie assured her. "I may take him away from you before you get him. Whoa! He isn't married, is he?"

Jenny shrugged and grinned foolishly. "How would I know? I don't even know his name."

Before the girls went to bed, Jenny remembered to tell

Charley they had to find a way to school tomorrow.

"No problem," Charley said. "We'll ride the cycle." Noting doubt creep over Jenny's face she continued, "Come on, roommate, I've ridden with you enough times." She tucked her hands into her armpits and flapped her elbows, cackling like a hen.

"OK," Jenny said laughing, "but only if you promise I'll come out of it alive. I don't mind admitting I hatched from an egg."

The next morning Jenny arrived at school wondering if she would ever be able to make herself look like a human. She began to understand Charley's wild fuzzy hair.

Charley took Jenny to the Ford dealer after school and marched up to the service desk for a look at Wonder Man.

When he saw Jenny he smiled and his dimples appeared, lighting his whole face. "All ready to go, Miss Cornell."

"What did you find?" Jenny asked after she caught her breath.

He shook his head. "The battery was a little low. Otherwise she's good as new."

"Are you saying nothing was wrong?" Jenny asked.

"I think the young man probably flooded it, then ground the starter until the battery failed. It's easy enough to do." He wrote something on a three-part invoice and handed Jenny the pink part. "We're just glad it's OK. No charge, of course."

When Jenny arrived home she found Charley sitting on the apartment steps, waiting for her. "He didn't have a wedding ring," Charley called before Jenny got out of the car.

The girls talked as they prepared vegetables for a stew. "What do you think?" Jenny asked.

Charley looked around. "About what?" she asked.

"You know. Him!"

Charley nodded. "I should have known. Well, he's all you said and more. Do you have your brand on him, or is it open season?"

Jenny laughed. "Probably neither of us will ever see him again."

"Yeah? We could rip something out of the car so it really won't work."

"Or get in a wreck," Jenny said, giggling.

Before school started the next morning a young teacher, Martin Mandell, wandered into Jenny's room. As he talked to Charley, Jenny mentally compared him to the service manager at Pendleton Ford. No contest, she decided. Martin was as blond as the other man was dark. His golden eyebrows and lashes were barely visible on his skin and his stomach nearly hung over his belt. When he laughed at a remark of Charley's his bright blue eyes and nice mouth brought it all together. He was pretty good-looking in his own way. And he made a nice friendly date. He'd taken Jenny out several times since school started a month ago.

He talked to Charley a few moments longer then strolled to Jenny's side at the chalkboard. "Hi, teacher," he said, looking her up and down.

"Hi, Martin, how's the fifth grade?"

He flashed his white teeth. "Oh, most of them know more than I, but I'm catching up. Speaking of catching up, I hear there's a hilarious new ballet Friday night at Vert." Vert Auditorium, Pendleton's all-purpose theater, also housed a museum.

"Sounds nice." Jenny loved music—if it wasn't rock. She'd played piano and sung a lot in high school and college productions.

"I'll pick you up at six o'clock and we'll have dinner

first." He walked away, swaying to an imagined rhythm.

Charley waited up for Jenny to return from her Friday night date. "How was it?" she asked breathlessly. "I've always wanted to go to one of those things—ballets."

Jenny popped onto her toes and did some pirouettes around the room, her arm curved gracefully over her head. "Fantastic. The meal was good, the music great, and the dancing out of this world." She stopped a moment then added, "And Martin is really nice."

Later, in bed, Jenny thought, *Why did I spend the entire evening thinking about the man from Ford? If I enjoyed Martin so much, how come the brown-eyed man kept trying to ruin my evening?*

Sunday afternoon Charley and Jenny took off in high spirits for LaGrande to have dinner with the Cornells. Jenny's folks wanted to meet their daughter's roommate and Jenny wanted Charley to meet her folks. "I have to warn you about my dad," Jenny said as they drove east on the freeway. "You never know what he's going to say, so you better be prepared for anything. I think he's the very happiest when he's embarrassing someone, preferably me."

After dinner, Jenny's mom, a short graying woman with a pleasant smile, expressed her approval of Charley. "I'm glad you have someone to share your apartment, Jenny. And to keep you from being so lonely," she added.

Charley laughed loudly. "Well, I do that, Mrs. Cornell."

"I don't hear much about your social life, though, dear," the woman continued. "Are you still going with that nice young teacher?"

"I'll bet your new roommate doesn't hang back from the men," Dad inserted before Jenny could answer. "She probably has your young teacher by now, huh, Jenny?" He raised his eyebrows twice to Charley and flicked ash off an imaginary cigar, in a poor imitation of Groucho Marx.

Jenny giggled. "I don't keep track of Charley's dates, Dad." She turned to her mother and continued, "I'm not *going* with him, Mom, but we still go places sometimes. We went to a ballet a few nights ago."

Mrs. Cornell nodded, satisfied.

Later, on the way home, Charley said, "How come you didn't tell your folks about him? Is he some sort of secret?"

"Don't be silly," Jenny said, chuckling. "There's nothing to tell." She leaned against the headrest and sighed. "Except that I think about him the first moment every morning and the last thing every night and every minute between." She glanced at Charley, relaxing beside her in the fading light. "Oh, yes. And dream about him while I sleep."

Charley smiled through her red lashes. "I knew that. You didn't fool me for a minute." Charley yawned a few times as they covered the miles between LaGrande and Pendleton. "Would you mind if I took a little nap?" she asked after a while.

"Sure, I don't mind driving alone. It gives me a chance to think."

Jenny sailed along the freeway, over the low hills and through the valleys. Finally she crested Cabbage Hill and saw the lights of Pendleton in the distance. Like Christmas lights twinkling in a dark window.

As she started up the next small rise the car didn't respond to her gas pedal. She punched it to the floor. Still nothing. She steered the car to the wide concrete shoulder, where it slowed to a stop.

Sleepily, Charley sat up. "We home already?" she asked.

Ignoring the question, Jenny turned the key in the ignition, giving the Mustang plenty of gas. It wouldn't catch. She kept churning until Charley snatched her hand and key from the ignition.

"Stop," she commanded.

Jenny felt alarm. "Why?" she asked, not attempting to reinsert the key.

"This is exactly what it did for Ward and me. Let it sit for a while. Maybe it'll start then."

A cold sweat appeared on Jenny's upper lip. Darkness had crowded out the last bit of daylight and sitting on the freeway at night didn't appeal to her in the least. A few cars whizzed past. Jenny hoped they would keep right on going.

Several hours later—her watch said ten minutes —Jenny tried to start the little red car again. After awhile she smelled gas fumes and the starter barely churned the engine.

"I think you better stop grinding on it," Charley said. "It looks as though we're due for a nice walk in the moon-light."

Jenny looked around. "From what moon?" she groaned.

Jenny worked on the starter until it made only a small click. She switched it off, leaned back, and dropped the key into her purse. "Well, so much for that." She grinned weakly at Charley. "What do we do now? We're a long way from nowhere."

"We walk. If we're lucky, someone picks us up and takes us to a telephone." Charlie chuckled and leaned to Jenny's ear. "Now do you believe Ward and I really had trouble?" she whispered.

"I already believed you, Charley. Well, almost. I'm sorry I treated you so mean." Jenny looked anxiously up the highway. "I don't want to ride with anyone cruising this highway. You never know who's in a car at night."

"I'd guess we're five miles from Pendleton," Charley

said, wide awake at last. "Are you up to a five-mile walk? And what're you going to do when a car passes, jump into the ditch?"

Jenny shuddered. Then she brightened. "Why don't we wait for a cop."

"I don't know," Charley said, "I've never seen one on this stretch, but if that's what you want."

"Have you thought about the good part?" Charley asked as they sat in the dark car, talking.

"No. How could there be a good part?"

Charley laughed loudly. "The man, Jenny. The Ford man. We'll get to see him again."

They discussed the price of seeing the man again, and whether it was worth it.

"Definitely, yes," Jenny decided.

After an hour had passed Charlie said, "What do you think, Jen? You want to stay here while I go for help? I'm not afraid, and you can lock the car doors."

"No, it'll be safer if we go together." Jenny put on her jacket, unlocked the door, and stepped out. Charley got out on the ditch side.

The traffic had thinned but cars flew past altogether too often to suit Jenny. Some people slowed then went on, probably as fearful of the girls as Jenny was of them. After half an hour, a car pulled up behind them. Jenny kept walking, her eyes pointed straight ahead. She grabbed Charley's hand and kept her going. "Don't you dare turn around," she gritted through her teeth.

A car door slammed. "Need some help?" a deep voice called.

Holding tightly to Charley's hand, Jenny put distance between them and the man as quickly as possible. The door slammed again and the engine started. Jenny didn't know whether to be happy or sad. But the car didn't leave.

It started toward them slowly. Then a siren sounded, emitting one small wail. Jenny whirled around to see a patrol car cruising slowly behind them, lights flashing.

As they watched, the car stopped and a uniformed officer stepped out, approaching in the illumination of his lights. "Are you ladies all right?" he asked again.

Charley let out a loud "Yahoo!" then glanced at Jenny. "Did you see the red Mustang back there, officer?" she yelled into the still night air.

"Sure did," he said. "You didn't think I'd pick up just any old hitchhikers, did you?" He laughed to let the girls know he was joking. "Come on, I'll take you into Pendleton."

Jenny called a tow truck, instructed them to take the Mustang to the Ford garage, then called a taxi. The buses had long since stopped running. Jenny fell into bed exhausted at 1:15 A.M.

The next morning the girls were nearly ready to leave for school on the motorcycle when the phone rang.

"This is Fletcher Leighton, Miss Cornell. I see we have your car with us again."

It took Jenny a moment to catch her breath—how did he do that to her? "Yes, it died on *me* this time," she said huskily a moment later. "Do you think you can have it fixed by afternoon?"

After a pause: "We'll certainly try. Could you tell me exactly what it did?"

"It died. In the middle of nowhere."

After school and a quick ride to the Ford dealer on the cycle, Jenny checked herself in the clean restroom. She applied fresh lipstick and brushed her hair.

"Why are you so particular?" Charley kidded. "You can see I didn't do anything special for him."

Jenny giggled. "All the better chance for me." She gave

the image in the mirror one last inspection. The dark hair feathered nicely back from her small face. Her pink lips turned up just the right amount, and the huge blue eyes looked unnaturally bright.

Jenny tried to see past the two men ahead of her at the service desk. Finally she stepped up to the chest-high counter. Even though she knew he would be there, she was unprepared for his clean good looks.

He dropped the key into her hand. "The car ran perfectly when we brought it inside this morning," he said.

"It couldn't!" She looked to Charley for reinforcement, then repeated quietly, "It couldn't."

"Yeah, that thing just shuts down," Charley added.

He shook his dark head, completely puzzled. "I had my best mechanic on it," he said. "He went completely through it. The battery was low again, so we replaced that. I think you'll be OK, now."

Jenny knew better. That battery had taken a lot of grinding.

"Hey," Charley said loudly, introducing a new subject. "I have some tickets to this great rock concert a week from Saturday." She raised her eyebrows. "What did you say your name is?"

"Fletcher Leighton. People call me Fletch."

Charley waved the tickets. "Want to go?"

He remained silent a moment. He brushed the curl off his forehead. "Sorry, I can't," he said. "But I have an idea. My church is sponsoring my favorite group, The Heritage Singers, that Saturday. They sing gospel music. I promised to help, so why don't you girls come as my guests?"

Jenny shook her head. She loved most music, but simply couldn't handle rock, not even gospel rock. "Sorry, that's not my style."

She couldn't believe her ears when Charley said, "I'll

go. What time is the concert—and where?"

"At the rodeo grounds at seven o'clock. Want me to pick you up?"

Charley shook her head. "Nah. I'll see you there. Thanks."

Fletch's deep brown eyes searched the depths of Jenny's bright blue ones. "Sure you wouldn't like to come?"

"I'm sure. I don't care for that kind of music." She turned to leave. "Thanks for all the work on the car," she flung over her shoulder.

"You're welcome. Hope it doesn't let you down again."

Jenny felt Fletch's eyes following her the whole 30-foot distance to the door. As she pulled the heavy door open, she heard a man's voice say, "That little one's a real fox, huh, Fletch?"

Jenny hesitated until the rich deep voice responded. "She's pretty all right, but she isn't for me."

3

Jenny rushed through the door and waited until it swung slowly shut. "Did you hear that?" she whispered.

"Hear what?" Charley asked loudly. "I guess I was thinking about Fletch's rock group. I've never heard of them. By the way, why didn't you go? You're the one who thinks he's so fantastic."

"Because I wouldn't look nice with my fingers in my ears, that's why." Red spots brightened Jenny's cheeks. "Charley, I just heard Fletch tell someone I wasn't for him. Why would he say that? I've felt strong vibes from the time we met. What could I have done?"

"Maybe he thinks you're too high and mighty, not liking rock music and all," Charley answered. "You probably don't speak the same language, sing the same song. You may even march to the beat of a different drummer." Her green eyes twinkled mischievously.

Fletch's remark kept troubling Jenny, although she didn't mention it to Charley again.

Jenny accepted another date with Martin and had a terrible time. Certain that he did, too, she decided she might as well stay home as make two people miserable. All she could think about at school, at home, or between, was what had she done to displease Fletch?

One morning everything went wrong and the girls left home 10 minutes late. They would still make it before school started, but Mr. Brock insisted that his teachers be half an hour early. Maybe they could sneak in without getting caught.

Jenny drove as fast as she dared, trying to make up the ten minutes. She shoved it into gear at a traffic light and felt that terrible *nothing*. As she pumped the throttle wildly, the motor quietly died. Cars piled up behind her, honking loudly.

"Whoa! What a horrible time to do it," Charley said, looking over her shoulder at the cars lining up behind them.

Jenny leaned her head on her arms on the steering wheel, making no effort to start the car. Why run the battery down again?

"Hey," Charley said, "why don't you run back to that guy behind us and tell him you'll honk his horn if he'll start your car?"

In no mood for jokes, Jenny ignored Charley's attempt to cheer her. "Why don't you run to a telephone and call a tow truck? I'll stay with the car. Call Mr. Brock, too." Charley jumped out, dodged two cars, and took off running.

What a mess, Jenny thought. *I'll be lucky if someone doesn't run over the car. On the other hand maybe I'll be luckier if someone does run over the beast.*

Jenny walked into her classroom half an hour late, her face red from embarrassment.

Charley followed, a sheepish look on her face. Mr. Brock stood before the class reading a book. When Jenny appeared, he slammed the book shut.

"Come with me, Miss Cornell," he snapped. "I need to speak to you."

"Would you start the students on their work, Miss Haywood?" Jenny asked, and followed her principal through the door.

She closed the door, took a deep breath, and leaned against the casing. "I'm sorry, Mr. Brock," she said, looking into the man's eyes, "my car quit on me. Miss Haywood called, didn't she?"

Mr. Brock emitted a long loud sigh. "No, Miss Haywood didn't call," he answered. "And frankly, Miss Cornell, I'm not concerned with your car. What I am concerned with are my students. I presume you'll take care of the problem so this doesn't happen again." He jerked his chin up twice and marched down the hall.

Jenny's breath came hard. Her face burned. She didn't need this. It wasn't as though she did it once a week. She shoved her hair back, took a deep breath, and opened the door to her classroom.

A little boy raised his hand as Jenny stepped behind her desk. "Yes, Tommy?"

He pointed to the top of the desk where Mr. Brock had unceremoniously dumped the book. "Are you going to finish the story?" he asked.

Jenny absently picked up the book. "I hadn't thought about it, Tommy," she said. "Did you enjoy Mr. Brock's reading?"

"No-o-o-o! He reads worse than I do."

A chorus arose. "Yeah!"

"He reads awful."

"My little brother reads better than him."

Jenny felt much better. She couldn't put the old grouch in his place, but she appreciated the kids doing it.

A little later, Leona Jones, the school secretary, stuck her head through the door, "Telephone, Miss Cornell."

Jenny laid down the lesson plan she was working on

and walked to the office with Leona, thankful the kids were at recess.

"This is Fletch Leighton, Jenny. Someone just told me your car is in the parking lot."

"Yes, it is, and I may never come after it," Jenny said quietly.

"That bad, huh? Did it cut out on you again?" Somehow his soft caring voice smoothed away some of the wrinkles Jenny had collected during that terrible morning.

"It cut out on me, all right. On a busy intersection. First and Court, to be exact." The humor of it finally hit Jenny and she began to laugh. "Oh, Fletch, you should have heard the irate drivers. And I caught a tongue lashing for being late for work. It hasn't been one of my better days."

"I'm sorry. I'll get it in right away and go through it myself. This has gone on too long. I'll try to have it ready after school."

Jenny beat her students back to the room, feeling better.

After school, Charley and Jenny took a bus across town to Pendleton Ford. When they walked in, they found no one at the service counter. "Maybe he's still working on it," Charley said. "Let's go out to the garage floor." They walked through the door and immediately spotted the Mustang in a stall at the far end.

Fletch stood beside the car, wiping his hands on a red rag. When the girls approached he shrugged and fanned his hands at his sides.

Jenny's good mood disappeared like last month's paycheck. "You mean you couldn't find anything?" she asked.

He shook his head. "It runs perfectly. I checked every part I thought it could be. Everything checked 100 per cent. It blows my mind. I have no doubt it will do it again, too."

Jenny felt helpless. "What can I do? Go on my way, knowing it will let me down any time? One more time on the way to school and I'll lose my job. Maybe I don't even want the car anymore."

Fletch wiped tools and put them away as they talked. "I don't blame you, Jenny, but I don't know what else to do at this point. If I could see it when it's not running I'm sure I could find it."

"Why don't you go for a drive with her?" Charley offered. "Maybe it'll quit on *you*." Charley smiled, looking pleased with herself.

Fletch shoved the rag under each fingernail, wiping hard. He glanced at Jenny, who wore a red face and said nothing.

He laid the rag down and stepped out of his coveralls. "Well, I could. If it conked out on me, I'm sure I could find the problem." He looked questioningly at Jenny, raising his eyebrows. "Think it would quit?"

"I have no idea."

"Take it up in the mountains," Charley suggested. "I guarantee it'll conk right out."

Jenny thought a moment. "I couldn't go before Saturday," she said. "How about Saturday?"

He shook his head. "How about Sunday? I'm free all day."

After agreeing on Sunday afternoon, Jenny and Charley left Fletch still folding coveralls and putting away the last of the tools. When the big door swung shut behind them Jenny said, "Why did you ever do that, Charley?"

Charley clapped Jenny on the back. " 'Cause you're such a chicken. You know you were dyin' to ask." Jenny turned her head so Charley's voice didn't strike her eardrums directly. She had learned it was less painful that way.

The next Sunday afternoon Jenny rummaged through her closet. "Charley," she said, "what should I wear?"

Charley skimmed Jenny's clothes and walked out of the room. Two minutes later she returned with an oversized baggy black sweater. Red, blue, and yellow diamonds scattered on the shoulder brought the front of the sweater to life. She handed it to Jenny. "Wear the yellow blouse and slacks," she said. "Put this over it. You'll look cuddly enough to kiss."

Jenny dropped her robe and climbed into the pre-scribed outfit. The huge sweater felt cuddly all right. "But I don't want to look cuddly enough to kiss," she said.

Charley roared with laughter. "Of course you do. I'm Charley, remember?" Then she took a long look at Jenny's face. "Want to borrow some eye shadow and lipstick? You always look sick."

"Thanks a lot, Charley," Jenny said, with a twinkle. "I have eye shadow and lipstick on."

When Fletch arrived, Jenny invited him to do the driving and they took off, with Jenny feeling a little edgy but eager for the afternoon.

After a brief silence while Fletch drove out of the city, he said, "This baby drives nice." He glanced at Jenny and shrugged. "Well, when it runs it drives nice."

Jenny nodded. "I know. I love the car when it behaves. I have to admit, though, I'd rather have an old junker that runs than a gorgeous new one that won't."

"You won't get an argument from me," Fletch said. "Nothing is so infuriating as an undependable car."

Jenny sat up straight and brushed her hair back. "Enough about cars. Where are we going?"

He shook his head. "I don't know. We're on the road to the mountains. Charley guaranteed the car would break down up there."

Jenny leaned back and relaxed. "Good. I love the Blues."

Fletch drove through the rolling wheatlands, not pushing the car. The young people relaxed, feeling constant conversation unnecessary.

After a little while curiosity overcame Jenny. "Tell me about yourself," she suggested.

Fletch shrugged, but smiled appreciatively. "There's not much to tell," he said. "I grew up right here in Pendleton. My two sisters are older than I. They're both married and have kids. I still live with my folks and probably will until I get married."

Jenny peeked at him from the corner of her eye. She wondered if he had someone picked out. Maybe that was why he said she wasn't for him. At least that made sense.

"Your turn," Fletch said, breaking the silence.

"Well, my family lives in LaGrande. I'm an only child. My parents were older when I was born. I graduated from Eastern Oregon State College last spring and now I'm learning to teach."

The car began to climb steadier as they approached the Blue Mountains, and the rolling fields gave way to low tree-covered hills. The air coming in through the open windows felt cooler.

Jenny wanted to ask Fletch if he had a girlfriend but that was more Charley's style. "Do you like your work?" she asked. There, no one could fault that question.

"I did. Until now, that is. I don't enjoy having a car we can't figure out." Fletch smiled at her and winked. "The car has humbled me," he added. "I always thought I was a pretty good mechanic."

Jenny felt like flying. *Come on, get hold of yourself, Jenny,* she told herself. *A wink is a far cry from a promise of undying love.* She still felt great. "You'll get it.

I just hope it doesn't do something else terrible before you find it."

Fletch laughed with her. "It's running well today. I hope Charley's a true prophet." Fletch looked at Jenny. "Would you like to stop at the Tamarack Inn for a cinnamon roll? They're the best."

"Sure," she said, "but I pay. You're donating your time. I hope?" She raised her eyebrows in a question and Fletch laughed.

"I'm donating my time and so are you," he said. "You're furnishing the car and gas. I furnish the food. Settled?"

Half an hour later, Fletch opened Jenny's car door and settled her back inside. "Do you ever ski up here?" he asked.

"No, I've never skied anywhere. Have you?" Jenny relaxed in the comfortable seat and fastened the shoulder harness.

The motor hummed as Fletch turned the key. "I ski anywhere I get a chance. Water and snow skiing are my favorite sports." He eased the car back onto the road. "Want to take a look at Langdon Lake?" he asked.

"Sure. It's one of my favorite places in the Blues."

In a little while they parked and walked to the water's edge. The lake sparkled with fall sunshine as the breeze teased the blue water into gentle waves. "Nice," Jenny said. She cuddled deeply into Charley's black sweater. "It's cool in the shade though."

Fletch indicated a rough bench beside the water. "Let's sit over here and talk a bit." After they were seated he tucked his sweater snugly around her. "Tell me your aspirations," he said.

Startled, Jenny had no answer. "I really don't know," she began. "I guess I want to get married and have a happy family like everybody wants and nobody gets."

"Do you feel that's an unattainable goal?" Fletch asked.

"I feel I'm getting cornered," Jenny said, laughing. "How about your own dreams?"

Fletch stood up abruptly with his back to her. He shoved his hands deep into his pockets and looked across the lake. "I guess I want to get married and have a happy family, too. And I know I can do it." He flung the words gently over the water. "But I want more. I'd like to help the people around me, not just my family, to have more joy in their lives." His voice trailed off and he stood silent.

Jenny stood beside him. "What a noble thought."

He smiled down at her and the dimples nearly caused her to choke. "There's more," he added. "What I want most of all is for my Saviour to return and take His people to the homes He has prepared for them."

In a little while they returned to the car. "Shall we take in Jubilee Lake while we're here? We take a left right here and it's about 12 miles."

Jenny checked her watch. Four-fifteen. "Sure. Why not?"

In a little while they pulled off at Jubilee Lake and enjoyed its beauty from the warmth of the car. A mother deer and nearly grown fawn walked boldly past the car to drink from the clear lake.

After a few minutes of friendly silence Fletch shoved the car into gear and wheeled around. "If we're destined for car trouble we should head home. Car trouble is easier to handle in the daylight."

"This car never goes for easy," Jenny said.

Fletch glanced at his watch. "It'll be dark before we get home, so it can do it in the dark if it wants."

Fletch drove moderately and they both enjoyed the fall colors—bright red vine maples against the quieter yellows and browns of the oaks and the dark evergreens. Jenny leaned forward, then relaxed. "Do you ever see bears up here?" she asked.

Fletch looked lazily down at her through his long dark lashes. "Nope. I'm sure they're up here, but they keep to themselves."

At that moment a new Ford pickup passed them as though they were walking. Fletch jerked his head from Jenny to the road. "Wow!" he said, watching the pickup, "that guy's moving. He must be in a hurry."

The man in the pickup must not be enjoying the trip as much as I am, Jenny thought, *or he'd drive very slowly.*

Suddenly Fletch pointed ahead. "Look!" he said, his voice thick. "Did you see that? The pickup left the road."

Jenny looked ahead and saw only a cloud of dust rising from the opposite side of the road. "Hurry," she whispered, her voice catching in her throat, "he may be hurt."

In a few seconds Fletch signalled, crossed the left lane and pulled off the road. Jenny jumped out and ran to the edge of the small embankment. The pickup lay on its side at the bottom, wheels spinning, and looking as though it had rolled several times. She saw no one.

In a few seconds Fletch stood beside her, looking with shock at the sight below. "I'm going down to see if I can help," he said. "You can stay up here if you'd rather."

Jenny didn't answer but stepped to the edge and began sliding slowly down the tall grass on the steep incline, grasping small bushes to slow her descent.

At the bottom, she ran and looked through the broken window. As she had suspected, the truck was empty. She looked in the grass nearby and found nothing.

Her huge blue eyes met Fletch's brown ones, both terrified. "We'll have to look farther from the truck," he said. "You look that way and I'll go over here." They tromped down the waist-high grass as they looked for the victim.

Jenny parted her millionth bunch of grass and found the man lying twisted and bruised. His pants were nearly torn off and blood gushed from a wound in his upper left leg. "Here he is," she shouted as she dropped to the wounded man's side. She unbuttoned his lightweight shirt and ripped it off him. Then she folded it and shoved it against the wound with all her strength.

Fletch stood behind her watching, wide eyed. "I'll go stop someone," he said and disappeared up the side of the bank.

Jenny looked the man over as well as she could without releasing the pressure on his leg. His left arm seemed to be lying at a strange angle and his face had very little skin left intact. His shallow breath came quickly and unevenly. No other dangerous amounts of blood were visible. She held the shirt hard on the wound.

She wondered if the man, probably in his mid-40s, was unconscious from the accident or from alcohol—she could smell it all over him.

Jenny heard sliding feet again and looked into Fletch's concerned eyes. "I stopped a guy in a truck," he puffed. "He radioed for help, so one of us better be up there to stop the ambulance." He knelt beside the injured man. "Here, let me do that. You go up and wait."

Jenny kept the pressure strong on the leg. "Where will the ambulance come from?" she asked.

"I'm not sure; maybe Walla Walla."

Jenny checked the shirt for blood once more. A little was seeping through but not much. "I'll hold it," she said, "but it'll be a while before the ambulance comes. Why don't you stay with me for a few minutes?"

Fletch settled quietly beside Jenny. No one said a

word. After a while the man began to struggle. Jenny's hand slipped from the wound and blood rushed into the shirt. Seeing this, Fletch grabbed the man and forced him back to a flat position. Jenny secured the shirt again and the bleeding stopped.

She heaved a big sigh. "Thanks," she mouthed to Fletch.

Then the man started vomiting.

4

The man tried to draw in a breath, choked, then vomited some more. Jenny motioned for Fletch to take the shirt. "Hold this," she said. "And don't let up on the pressure." She quickly turned the man's head all the way to one side. Then she opened his mouth and scooped out the vomit with her hand. As it came up she cleared it out, all the way back to his throat. The putrid smell made her feel faint, and it felt lumpy —and slimy. Her stomach tried to flip but she couldn't allow that. The man would die if she didn't help him breathe.

As she frantically worked to keep his mouth clear she heard a siren. It increased in volume as it neared, then slowed to a stop. A door slammed and two men scrambled down the embankment. Jenny gladly backed away when the men approached. One of them began working on the man and the other scrambled up the hill, returning moments later with equipment. Fletch kept the pressure on the leg.

The medic pushed a tube down the man's throat. "Looks like you saved a life here," he said without looking up.

No one answered.

In a little while they took the leg from Fletch and put a pressure bandage on it, then splinted the arm.

"OK, let's transport," one of them said. "We'll need your names and addresses." They strapped the man onto a stretcher and carried him up the hill and into the ambulance.

Fletch handed them the paper with the requested information. The big motor throbbed and the siren wailed as the ambulance took off. The lettering on the ambulance said *Pendleton*.

Jenny leaned on the car, totally spent. Her stomach began to roll and saliva accumulated in her mouth. Oh, no! She was going to be sick after all. She dropped onto the rocks beside the car.

Fletch ran to her side. "Are you all right, Jenny?" he asked.

Unable to answer, she leaned her head over her knees and kept swallowing. She simply couldn't vomit now.

Fletch squatted beside her and awkwardly patted her back. After a time that seemed forever the saliva stopped coming and her stomach settled down. She looked at Fletch, one side of her mouth twisting into an embarrassed smile.

He waited a little longer. "Would you like to go now?" he finally asked softly. "Or do you need a little more time?"

She shook her head. "I think I'm all right." Her eyes met his. His eyes looked so soft, caring, filled with love.

Fletch took Jenny's arms and helped her to her feet, then gently put her into the car. He ran around and jumped in. Then they headed down the mountain toward home.

Jenny rested quietly. As she felt better she became aware of a horrible stench. She looked around, then discovered the smell came from her! Nasty smelling vomit mixed with blood covered her—Charley's—sweater. She unfastened the seat belt, pulled the sweater off, rolled it up, and shoved it under the seat. Her yellow blouse felt wet and smelled too, but not quite so badly.

She peeked at Fletch. He flashed her one of his best smiles, his dimples deep and sexy. She swallowed once more. "I'm sorry," she whispered.

He looked surprised. "What could you possibly be sorry about?"

She shrank into herself a little more. "For stinking up the car," she whispered again.

He laid his head back and laughed. "Forget it." Then he grew serious. "Have you had nursing training?" he asked.

She shook her head. "No." After a moment she continued in a small choked voice. "I just did what I had to. And then I got sick." They rode quietly into Pendleton and up King Avenue to Jenny's apartment. When she got out she remembered the reason for their trip. "The car didn't break down," she said.

He smiled tenderly at her. She saw that wonderful look in his eyes again. If it wasn't love at least it was loving. But then his expression became veiled and he turned away, as though he didn't want her to know how he felt.

"No, the car didn't break down, but the day wasn't wasted. The Lord sent us into the mountains today, Jenny, to do a job for Him."

He took a long breath. "And Jenny, you were simply wonderful." He jumped into his car, waved, and drove off.

Jenny stumbled into the house. After she had a long hot shower and shampooed her hair twice, she told Charley about the accident. "I'm so sorry about the sweater," she said. "I'll buy you a new one."

Charley waved the thought away. "I never buy clothes that can't be washed," she said. "That sweater has had worse things on it than blood and barf. Tell me about Fletch. What do you think about him now?"

Jenny's eyes glowed and her face took on a dreamy look. "He's fantastic, Charley, and he likes me too. I'm sure he's forgotten what he said about me not being for him." She pulled her knees up and hugged them as she sat on the couch. "Oh, Charley," she said, "I wish you could have seen the way he looked at me."

Jenny called St. Anthony's hospital and felt relieved to learn the man would be all right. She went to bed with happy thoughts of Fletch dancing through her mind. Once or twice she saw his dark eyes become veiled, but pushed the image away.

Jenny lived in a rosy glow the next few days waiting for Fletch to call. She knew he wanted to see her again as badly as she wanted to see him. But the days tiptoed past, one at a time, and he didn't call. The police interviewed her about the accident, then the weekend came and she still hadn't heard a word. She couldn't understand it.

"Come on, Jenny," Charley begged, Saturday afternoon. "At least you'll see him at the concert. You know he'll be there."

Jenny shook her head. "I'm not like that, Charley, and you know how much I dislike rock music."

"No, you're not like that." Charley shook her wild red hair. Her blue-lidded green eyes weren't laughing. "You're from the dark ages, Jenny, and it's time to climb out."

As Charley disappeared in the roar of her motorcycle, Jenny wished she'd had the courage to go. There was something to be said for Charley. She had the guts to go after what she wanted. Not that she wanted Fletch. For some reason he didn't turn Charley on as he did Jenny.

As she spent the longest, loneliest evening of her life, Jenny thought about things. Fletch said they hadn't come upon the wreck by accident. She wondered. Anyway, she felt glad that they had saved the man's life. She called the hospital again and found that the man was progressing nicely.

She wondered if she'd ever see Fletch again. The car had run perfectly all week. Maybe it had healed itself. She smiled as she realized how dumb it was to wish for car trouble.

For some strange reason, Fletch really didn't intend to get involved with her. Maybe he was engaged. He had never made an improper move toward her. Just a kind mechanic trying to help out. But that one unguarded look. An engaged man would never look at another woman like that—unless he shouldn't be engaged!

After a time that seemed forever the big cycle roared into the garage and a moment later Charley burst through the back door. "It was fantastic, Jenny. You should have been there." She flopped onto the carpet beside the couch.

Jenny waited a moment while Charley basked in her memories. "Well," Jenny said at last, "aren't you going to tell me about it?"

Charley opened her blue eyelids wide. "Why? I thought you weren't interested." Then she laughed at 78 decibels. "Yes, he was there. But he was with a gorgeous girl."

Jenny's heart landed in her throat, cutting off her breath. She swallowed. She could still feel the thing beating hard against her windpipe. If she could only breathe. She swallowed again but the lump didn't go away. Why should she be surprised? Hadn't she guessed a girl was the reason he said she wasn't for him?

Charley laughed again. "Jenny, why the red face? You don't care who he goes with, do you?"

Jenny still couldn't respond.

Charley peered into Jenny's face. "Oh, Jen," she said, "I'm sorry. The girl really was darling. He brought her over to meet me, but she was 3 years old. She was his niece, Jen, and she wasn't really with him. He worked through the whole concert, setting up equipment, running the sound, doing everything that needed doing." She brushed a red-tipped finger under Jenny's eyes. "Now see what I did," she said. "I made you cry."

At last Jenny's heart beat steadily in her chest where it belonged and she felt able to talk again. "It's OK, I'm just tired. Did you like the music?"

Charley's head swayed back and forth before she answered. "I loved it." She looked at Jenny and shook her head. "But it wasn't rock. I just wish you'd been there."

Jenny wished she'd been there, too. "I'll go next time," she said.

Charley shook her head. "They won't be back until next fall."

"Did Fletch mention me?" Jenny didn't want to ask, but couldn't help it.

Charley hesitated, then barely moved her head sideways. "Sorry, Jen. But he was real busy."

Well, so much for that. Jenny would simply put Fletch out of her mind. No need tearing herself up over someone who had no interest in her. She'd never had trouble finding friends among the opposite sex. She'd just get so busy she wouldn't have time to think about him. She went to bed and thoughts of Fletch kept her mind so active she couldn't fall asleep.

After school on Monday, Charley and Jenny went grocery shopping. "Hey, did I tell you I met a neat guy at the concert?" Charley asked.

Jenny weighed six Granny Smith apples. She shook her head. "No, tell me," she said, her mind on the high cost of food.

Charley laughed loudly and several nearby shoppers glanced at the girls. "Are you ready for this, Jen? He's an inch or two shorter than I, but oh, is he ever gorgeous! Black hair, eyes, and mustache."

Charley had Jenny's attention now. She stopped, her hands resting on the cart, and looked at Charley. "How'd you meet the guy, anyway?" she asked.

Charley raised her eyebrows and looked mysterious. She shoved her hair away from her face. "Fletch introduced us. His name is Adam Stanwick and he's a lot friendlier than Fletch. Prettier, too."

Jenny doubted that with all her heart. "Fletch is friendly enough," she said. "He just doesn't—well—I guess he isn't friendly enough. Did this guy—what's his name?—invite you out?"

Charley put her hand on the cart and started it down the aisle again. "No, he didn't ask me out, but he came back to talk to me several times. He asked my name twice, too. He'll call."

The girls put their attention to the shopping and in a little while arrived at home. Charley put the groceries away while Jenny started cooking supper. "Good luck on the guy calling, Charley," Jenny said. "I know Fletch is never going to call me. I'm going to stop thinking about him and go with anyone who asks."

Charley closed the refrigerator door and turned to Jenny with a bright look. "Maybe you'd like to go with Ward," she said.

Jenny shook her head. "No way. He looks about 16."

Charley gave Jenny a strange look. "So do you. If you'd wear a little more makeup, you'd look more mature." She found the apples and reopened the refrigerator door. "Anyway I was just trying to find a way not to hurt Ward."

"How are you going to hurt him?" Jenny wanted to know.

Charley pulled her head out of the refrigerator and

shook it in disbelief. "Jenny, you haven't heard a word I said. I'm in love with Adam Stanwick and he won't want me going with someone else."

Jenny laughed. "Oh Charley, you're priceless. But don't dump Ward until Adam calls, OK?" Several days passed and neither Fletch nor Adam called. Neither girl mentioned the men, but both waited.

One afternoon after Jenny dismissed her class, a large blond man appeared in the doorway. His size caused Jenny to give him a quick second look. He must have been closer to seven feet tall than six. His shoulders looked as broad as any football player's—and his muscular chest melted into a tiny waist and hips. "Miss Cornell?" he asked.

"Yes, come in."

He walked to the desk where Jenny sat, pulled a chair close and sat down. He shoved a huge hand over the desk to her. "I'm Vince Rogers," he announced proudly.

Vince Rogers. Was she supposed to know who that was? Oh, oh, oh. Maybe she did. She accepted the hand and shook vigorously. "Is Annie Rogers a relative of yours?" she asked.

The man straightened his shoulders. "She's my daughter."

"Annie's a doll, Mr. Rogers, and a fantastic student, but is there a problem?"

The man stood up and Jenny noticed lint balls covered his worn gray sweater like snow flakes on a bare field. It was clean, though, and what a body! He must be a weight lifter.

"No problem, Miss Cornell," Vince Rogers said. "Annie has chosen you for her new mother. Good choice, too." He looked Jenny over from her soft dark hair past her long-lashed deep-blue eyes, high cheek bones and straight narrow nose, to her red ruffled blouse and white pants.

He nodded thoughtfully.

Jenny's face reddened. "I—I—wasn't aware that Annie didn't have a mother," she stammered.

The man gracefully returned his bulk to the chair. "I'm sorry, Miss Cornell, I didn't mean to embarrass you." He shook his golden hair and his blue eyes crinkled at the corners. "Would you consider going to a movie with me soon? Like tonight?"

A dark-haired, dark-eyed face smiled gently in her mind and the dimples twinkled like flashing lights. *Oh, Fletch,* her heart cried, *how can I go with anyone else when I love you.* Love! She loved Fletch? How could she love Fletch? She didn't know him well enough to love him. She didn't know whether to laugh or cry at the thoughts racing through her mind. She wasn't any more mature than Charley.

Her mind returned to the man sitting across from her, waiting for an answer. She attempted a friendly smile. "Well, Mr. Rogers, I don't know. I've never been selected for a mother before."

Vince Rogers laughed—a deep, gentle laugh. "I should never have said that, Miss Cornell, but I haven't asked a woman out for 12 years. Could we just erase that dumb remark and start over?"

Jenny could barely hear the man over her heart shouting, *You love Fletch! I don't!* she shouted back. *And Fletch certainly doesn't love me.* "Why don't we just turn this into a meeting discussing Annie?" Jenny said, aloud. "She really doesn't have any problems at school. She's a darling child and wonderful student. You must be doing something right to have such a well-adjusted daughter."

A wide smile reached Vince's eyes. "Yeah, she's OK. I guess that's why I listened when she insisted I meet you." He grinned and rubbed his chin with a monstrous paw.

"She's been at me since the middle of September, Miss Cornell, and I'll be in trouble if I don't have anything to report."

Jenny stood up and offered her hand again. "Well, let's not get you in trouble. You tell Annie we'll all get together soon, but not tonight. Good-bye, Vince, I must go now."

Jenny caught Charley's eye with a silent signal for help. Charley shoved her jaw to one side and raised her eyebrows. Folding the papers she'd been grading, she carried them to Jenny's desk.

Jenny draped an arm around Charley's waist. "This is my favorite helper, Vince, Charlene Haywood."

Vince stood to his feet and glanced at Charley. "Yeah. Well, good-bye, Miss Cornell. You'll be hearing from me soon."

After he closed the schoolroom door Charley leaned back and ogled Jenny. " 'Yeah, well, good-bye, Miss Cornell,' " she mimicked in a voice an octave lower than normal. She shoved Jenny in a friendly way. "Honestly, Jen, I'm not going to be seen with you, anymore." Her green eyes sparkled like early morning dew on a lush lawn. "Know why? Because if you're around they don't see me!"

She cackled at full volume as the girls walked down the hall and out to Jenny's car. "And I'd call that guy the hunk of hunks, wouldn't you?" she asked. "Too bad we're both already in love."

Charley brought up the subject of the big man again at supper. "You aren't really thinking of going out with King Kong, are you?"

Jenny chewed her raw carrot and swallowed. "You know something, Charley? It felt kind of nice for someone to find me attractive. Obviously Fletch doesn't." She snatched a slice of bread and buttered it, using long hard strokes.

Charley shook her head as though disappointed. "You know your problem, Jen?" she asked. Then she answered her own question. "Your problem is that you aren't aggressive. You lie down like an overcooked noodle. Well, I'm not going to do that."

"No?" Jenny doubted that Charley could think of any way to get Adam's attention. "What are you going to do?"

Charley laid her fork in her plate and wiped her mouth with a napkin. Then she stood to her five feet seven and a half inches. "I'm going to call Fletch and find out more about Adam." She turned her green eyes full on Jenny. She sniffed and stuck her nose in the air. "I told you I was aggressive."

Jenny's heart pounded out approval, but aloud she said, "I don't think you should do that." Head over heart, she told herself.

Charley marched to the phone and looked up Fletch's number.

"Hi, Fletch," she began cheerily, "this is Charley." Pause. "Charlene Haywood." Pause. "Jenny Cornell's friend." She looked at Jenny and shook her head, and rolled her green eyes. "Yes, the red head. I was just wondering if you could tell me about Adam Stanwick."

"Dumb guy," she mouthed to Jenny.

"What do I want to know? Well, does he have a girlfriend and where could I see him again?" Long silence. Then she nodded. "All right! Thanks a lot, Fletch. See you." She hung up, slapped her leg, and sat back down at the table, grinning as though she'd seen the tooth fairy.

After waiting a reasonable time Jenny said, "Well?"

"Well," Charley began, "Fletch told me how to see Adam again and you can see Fletch, too."

Jenny shook her head. "You don't catch on. I don't want

to see Fletch unless he wants to see me. Where do you see Adam?"

"At their church. He told me to go to prayer meeting tomorrow night. Come on, Jen, I need you for moral support."

Jenny jumped up and started clearing away the dishes. "No way. You're the little Sunday school girl. You'll be all right." She opened the dishwasher door and began filling it. "I would like to see this Adam guy though. Bring him home after the meeting."

Jenny tried to think about Vince the next day, but Fletch crowded all else from her mind. *I guess the only way to get rid of him is to replace him,* she decided. She wrote a note to Vince and gave it to Annie to take home. The note said: "Let's take Annie to a movie Saturday afternoon. Jenny Cornell." She drove home feeling pretty bold, though unexcited; she didn't mention it to Charley.

Jenny was relaxing on the couch that evening when Charley came out of her bedroom, ready for her trip to church.

Jenny hopped lightly to her feet and took Charley's hand. "Come on into my bedroom," she said, "and let me help with your make-up."

Charley jerked her chin an inch higher. "Don't try to take me back into the dark ages," she snapped. "Are you sure you aren't a secret agent for my old church?"

"Sorry," Jenny said quietly. "I was only trying to help."

Charley sparkled again. "Come with me, Jen. Please?"

Jenny motioned the girl out the door. "He'd know I went only to see him."

Alone, Jenny tried to think of something exciting to do. She really had wanted to go with Charley. She washed a load of clothes and put them into the dryer. Then the guy in the accident popped into her head. She picked up the phone and called St. Anthony's Hospital. Yes, the man was still there. Before she had time to change her mind she piled into the Mustang and drove down the hill to the hospital.

After getting the room number, Jenny walked up the stairs and down the hall and peeked into the man's room. He lay propped up in his bed, reading a magazine. "Hello there," she said, walking to the bed. "You look about 2,000 percent better than the last time we met."

The man raised his eyebrows and looked her over. "Hello yourself," he said. "Am I supposed to know you?"

Jenny laughed. "No, I guess you wouldn't. But I know you. I had my arm down your throat after your accident."

The man sat a little straighter and stuck his good hand out, cranking Jenny's up and down. "Yeah! I heard about you. Thanks. I heard you were into my leg, too. They said I'd have bled to death if you hadn't been there. Choked to death, too." He relaxed on his pillow a moment then added, "I'm sure glad you have two arms." He looked down at his own arm, encased in a cast from the end of his fingers to his shoulder.

Jenny laughed with him. "I did only what anyone else would have done. And I didn't use both arms at once. A really great guy held your leg most of the time."

"I guess that's me, great guy and all." Fletch walked in with dimples flashing—and Jenny felt faint.

C H A P T E R

5

Fletch carried two news magazines and a chocolate milkshake. "Don't you believe her for a minute. She saved you. How are you, Steve?" He laid the magazines on the table and handed the milkshake to the man in bed.

He turned to Jenny and smiled. The dimples flashed again and Jenny's stomach did a triple somersault. "How is our little Florence Nightingale?" he asked.

Jenny's face warmed. "Stop that," she said, smiling. "We worked together to help someone in need. That's all there was to it."

The man on the bed, Steve, sucked loudly on his milkshake, shook the container, then waved his hand. "Hey, Florence Nightingale, that's not what the man told me." He winked at Fletch. "You weren't too far off on her looks, either."

Apparently sensing Jenny's discomfort, Fletch changed the subject. "Steve Sawyer, I gather you haven't formally met Jenny Cornell."

"How are you, Steve?" Jenny asked with a friendly smile.

"Physically, I'm fine. The big problem is in my pocket. They really nailed me for driving under the influence."

Jenny cast a quick look at Fletch, not knowing what to

say. She felt strongly about drunk driving, and no fine could be stiff enough as far as she was concerned.

Fletch laughed. "Well, Steve, when we found you, you weren't feeling any pain."

Steve looked sober. "I can tell you one thing. I'm never going to drink and drive again."

"Good idea," Fletch agreed, nodding his dark head. "The only thing better would be for you not to drink again, period."

"Well, I better be going," Jenny said, easing toward the door. "My roommate will be home and wonder where I am. By the way, Fletch, I thought you'd be at church tonight."

"Nope. I knew Steve was leaving tomorrow, so thought I'd rather spend some time with him." He walked out with Jenny. "Be back in a minute," he called over his shoulder.

"I wouldn't if I were in your place," Steve returned jovially.

In the hall, Fletch looked into Jenny's eyes. "You're pretty nice," he said quietly. "Did you know that?"

"I am?" she asked in surprise. And before she could stop herself she added, "I thought you didn't think so."

Fletch stepped in front of Jenny and put his fingers under her chin, tipping it up. "Where did you ever get an idea like that?" His eyes had that look again. For just a moment. Then the veil fell firmly in place again.

And how could she answer his question? She couldn't say it was because he hadn't called. That's what Charley would say. She raised her eyes to his soft brown ones, trying to smile casually. "Oh, just a hunch, I guess."

Here came the dimples again, running over Jenny like a loaded freight train. He hesitated, then shrugged. "Well, so much for hunches," he said. "I better get back in there." He retraced the few steps into Steve's room.

The lights were on when Jenny stepped onto her

kitchen porch. Charley met her at the door. She reached out and jerked Jenny inside. "Was it that bad?" Jenny asked.

"It was fantastic. And Adam kept looking at me all evening."

"Did he ask you out?"

"No, but I could tell he wanted to. A lot of people gathered around and talked. They're real friendly." Charley followed Jenny to her room and sat on the frilly pink bedspread. "It reminded me a lot of my church. And it made me feel good. I'm going back next week, Jen. Will you go?"

Jenny started removing her makeup. "I told you I'm not going, Charley. I'm not giving Fletch the satisfaction of chasing him."

"He wasn't even there, Jen."

Jenny smiled wryly. "I know. We were together." She told about her visit to the hospital. She didn't mention Fletch telling her she was nice.

Friday night Jenny answered the phone to hear a strange male voice ask for Charley.

"Yes, when?" Charley asked. "Sure, I'd love to. See you then." She hung up the phone and turned shining eyes to Jenny. "That was Adam. Did I tell you he wanted to take me out or what?"

Jenny smiled at Charley's transparent happiness. "You told me. Where are you going—and when?"

Charley's eyes sparkled. "We're going to church. To-morrow morning at 9:15."

"Tomorrow's Saturday."

Charley grinned and shrugged, tipping her head to one side. "I guess they must be Seventh-day Adventists, Jen."

When Charley returned from church the next day, Jenny was dressing for her movie date with Vince and

Annie, not looking forward to it much but glad she'd invited Annie.

"I loved the service," Charley said, bouncing into Jenny's room. "I think I've missed church a lot. It did seem strange to be sitting in church on Saturday, though. They call it the Sabbath," she added as an afterthought.

"Are you going again?" Jenny slipped into a soft pink sweater and black pants.

"He's taking me to prayer meeting Wednesday night."

"Wow, this sounds serious."

The doorbell interrupted and Jenny hurried to open it. Vince, filling the whole doorway, wore the same sweater he'd worn to school, and faded jeans. "Hey," he said, "don't you look pretty!"

Jenny lifted her light jacket from the couch and walked out with him. He walked to his side of the old pickup while Jenny walked to her own door. She tried the door but nothing happened. He leaned across and opened it and she climbed in.

"You have to open it from the inside," he explained, shoving the key into the ignition.

"Hey, where's Annie?" Jenny asked, realizing the little girl was not in the truck. "This day was for her."

He started the truck, rammed it into gear, and pulled into the street. "She had something else to do," he said.

They went to a kid's movie and Jenny felt terrible that Annie wasn't there to enjoy it. During the movie Vince slipped his arm across the back of her seat. Jenny leaned forward. Then he dropped the arm on her shoulder and pulled her close. She tried to move away but he held her tightly. She reached up and shoved his hand off her shoulder and jerked away hard. His hand fell behind the seat with a thud. He put it in his lap and sat quietly.

Jenny heaved a sigh of relief when the movie ended

and they eased out with the crowd.

As Vince drove home he looked at Jenny. "I suppose you're wondering how I ended up with the kid," he said.

As Jenny thought about it, she did wonder what type of tragedy left this man trying to be mother and father to a little girl. She smiled kindly. "Only if you want to tell. I'm sure it hurts you to talk about it," she said.

"Naw, it don't hurt anymore." He wiped his forehead with a large handkerchief he brought from his pocket. His blond hair and blue eyes really were quite attractive. He looked as though he worked outside, too, judging by his deep tan.

"Used to, though. Old lady took off with her boss. They didn't want a kid around, messing up their life. Simple, huh?" Vince glanced at Jenny, then steered the old truck around a corner.

"How awful—for you and Annie, too. When did this happen?"

He gazed into space a moment. "About four years ago, I guess. Long enough for us to be used to it by now." He held his arm straight out the window, signalling a left turn. "Still gets kinda lonely sometimes," he added in a soft voice that contrasted his massive size.

Jenny felt his pain and hurt with him. When he pulled into Jenny's driveway it became obvious he wasn't going to walk her to the door so she jumped down and walked around to his window. "Would you and Annie like to come for dinner some night soon?" she asked.

He jerked his head up and down ecstatically. "I'd like that. Neither of us is a very good cook."

"OK, thanks for the nice time today. How about Monday night at six o'clock? And Annie has to come too. I mean that."

"Sure. Thanks. See you Monday." He waved out the

window all the way to the corner.

Monday afternoon after school Jenny and Charley hurried to the supermarket to pick up last minute items. Back in the car, Jenny hurried as fast as she dared. She wanted everything nice tonight. Why couldn't she be making this dinner for Fletch? No, no, no. She really wanted to help make Annie's life a little happier. She'd gotten some Popsicles just for the little girl.

She felt someone pound her on the shoulder. Oops, the light had turned green. "Jen, are you there?" Charley asked. "I wondered if you'd like for me to leave tonight. I'd be glad to."

Jenny pulled into the intersection, then grinned at her friend. "I told you I want you *not* to leave tonight. The more the better. Annie's going to be there and I want you there, too."

About mid-block, a car stopped short in front of them and Jenny slammed on the brakes. Then when she stepped on the accelerator nothing happened. She pumped frantically, with no results. Nothing. "It's done it again," she screamed. "Now what are we supposed to do?"

Charley leaned back in the seat and laughed—loud and long.

"What could possibly be funny?" Jenny asked her convulsive roommate.

Charley struggled for control a moment, then said, "Do you really want to have that guy for dinner tonight?"

"Of course I don't," Jenny said. "But I invited them —and now we won't be ready."

Charley still laughed. "Guess who you get to see first?"

Oh! She'd get to see Fletch. But she didn't have time to see Fletch! Drat that car. Why did it have to pick an evening when she was so busy?

"Well, don't just sit there," Charley said. "Let's go find

a phone and call your personal mechanic."

"Before the Popsicles melt," Jenny said, climbing out of the spiteful red beast.

"Oh no. I'm so sorry," Fletch said when he heard what had happened. "I'm up to my shoulders in work but I'll send a truck and someone to take you home."

What! He couldn't even take the time from his precious work to help her? He didn't care about the car and he didn't even want to see her. "Well, get him here in a hurry," she said with more emphasis than necessary, "I have a guy coming for dinner tonight and I want it to be perfect!" She slammed down the receiver, hoping it broke Mr. Wonderful's eardrums.

A new blue Taurus arrived in five minutes and a young kid, dressed in a Ford uniform, hopped out. "May I take you ladies home?" he asked with a friendly smile.

After the food was loaded, Charley sat in front and visited with the young man. "I'm sorry you're upset," he said to Jenny, after carrying the groceries in. "Mr. Leighton told me about your trouble. He said you're to take me back to the garage and use the Taurus until your Mustang is fixed."

"Tell him to keep the Taurus," Jenny said. "We don't have time to go after it. And as for the Mustang, those jerks don't know anything about fixing a car. They might as well just tow it here."

The young man looked doubtful. "All right, if you're sure you don't want the car." He gave Charley a friendly smile and turned away. "Have a nice dinner," he called as he ran back to the Taurus.

Charley draped a friendly arm around Jenny's neck. "Sorry you're so disappointed you didn't get to see him, Jen, but you will tomorrow."

Jenny took a quick breath. Charley was right. Because

Fletch had hurt her gave her no excuse to turn on everyone else. She better straighten up and make it a happy evening.

The meal steamed on the stove, the table was set, and both girls had had time for a shower when the doorbell announced the guests. Charley opened the door while Jenny stirred the gravy. "Hi, Vince, come in. We're all ready."

Charley bustled into the kitchen and Vince leaned against the doorway. His massive frame, in the same sweater and jeans, dwarfed the comfortably sized kitchen. He sniffed. "Mmmm. Smells good enough to eat—and I'm starved."

"Hey, where's Annie?" Jenny asked.

He dropped his gaze. "Well, she wasn't feeling great so I thought she better not come."

"She felt just fine when she left school this afternoon, Vince." Jenny heard her voice rising again. "She was looking forward to this evening, too." *Calm yourself, Jenny. It's not Vince's fault you didn't see Fletch.*

He studied the refrigerator door handle. "Well, you see, it sort of came on her sudden like." He slowly raised his eyes to meet Jenny's. "She'll be fine. She just needed a little extra rest."

Jenny turned off the burner and laid down the spoon. "Get her, Vince," she said. "We aren't eating until you do."

"But she's already eaten."

"I don't care. I expressly invited Annie, and you'd better get her. Who's with her, anyway?"

"Oh, she isn't that sick," Vince said with conviction. "She don't need anyone to stay with her."

"What? You don't leave an 8-year-old child alone, even when she's well. Come on, Vince, we're going after Annie." Jenny marched out the door to Vince's beat-up pickup truck. Reaching through the open window, she unlatched the door and climbed in.

A few minutes later Jenny ran up the steps behind Vince into the old house. Inside, they found Annie sitting on a sagging couch, watching TV. Her tear-stained face looked apprehensive when she saw the two of them. "Why are you home so soon, Daddy?" she asked, her voice trembling.

"Miss Cornell didn't believe you're sick, princess. You tell her."

Jenny looked into Annie's pathetic blue eyes. The child remained silent. Jenny spread a big smile across her face and put her hand out to the child. "Come on, Annie, we're taking you to dinner."

The child looked at her father. "Tell her you've already eaten, Annie," Vince said.

Annie looked at Jenny and nodded. Jenny sat down beside Annie and drew her close. "What did you eat?" she asked.

Annie hesitated and glanced at her father. "I didn't eat, Miss Cornell," she stammered, "my supper is on the table."

Jenny walked into the kitchen where a slice of bread and peanut butter lay hardening on the bare table. A couple of cabinet doors hung open and she noticed bare shelves. "Is this it?" she asked, touching the bread.

Annie nodded. "I wasn't hungry."

"I told you she didn't feel well," Vince insisted.

Jenny forced a happy laugh. "Well, come on, you guys, the dinner is getting cold at my house."

Annie looked at her father and he nodded. The little girl scampered to Jenny and clung tightly to her hand.

Home again, Jenny and Charley had the meal on the table in a few minutes. And Annie ate as though she were starved.

"The food is fantastic," Vince said, as Charley gave him a second piece of fresh peach pie. He smiled appreciatively at Charley. "Did you make it?"

Charley laughed. "As a matter of fact I did. This is one of my better creations. My cooking doesn't always turn out." Charley had a second piece, too, and insisted Annie have another.

Jenny didn't eat much. She spent her mealtime wondering about Annie and Vince. Maybe they didn't have money to buy decent food. She'd find out. Somehow.

Annie asked to watch a rerun of *Three's Company*, so the little group watched John Ritter's foolishness. Charley and Annie screamed in laughter at the actor's antics.

Then the telephone rang.

"This is Fletch, Jenny. We went through the car with the usual results. It's running fine." He sounded truly sorry, but Jenny chose not to hear it.

"So what else is new?" she asked.

"I just wondered if you'd like me to drop it off now, or should we do some more searching in the morning?"

She sighed. How could he always remain so calm—and so nice? "Whatever you think," she said quietly. "Are you likely to find the cause of the trouble if you try again?"

A short silence. Then an audible sigh. "I wish I could say yes, but I'm not very optimistic."

Jenny couldn't resist the chance to see him. "Why don't you drop it by tonight, then?" After a moment's silence she added, "I'm sorry I was unkind, Fletch. I know this isn't your fault."

A little later Fletch dropped Jenny's keys into her hand and stuck his head through the door, frankly checking out her company.

"Won't you come in for a little while?" Jenny asked.

Fletch flushed, obviously embarrassed at his behavior.

"OK," he said, "for a little while."

The conversation centered around the Mustang's mysterious ailment. When Vince heard about the trouble, he wanted to fix it. "I can fix anything on wheels," he said, nodding in emphasis.

"I'd appreciate your input, Vince," Fletch said earnestly. "That car has us babbling in our sleep."

After a little while Annie got tired and Vince reluctantly took her home.

Fletch leaned back in the recliner and eased his eyes through his long dark lashes until he met Jenny's. "So that's the boyfriend," he said ever-so-casually.

Jenny felt tempted to say, Yes, isn't he wonderful? But her innate honesty wouldn't allow it. Besides, she needed some good advice and somehow she trusted Fletch's judgment.

She shrugged and smiled into Fletch's soft eyes. "No, just the father of one of my students." She leaned forward. "I'm a little concerned about them."

"They looked all right to me. What could be causing your concern?"

"Well, it's mostly just a feeling, but somehow I think they're having financial problems." She told him about the peanut butter sandwich and empty cabinets.

"Did you say the girl is well-adjusted?" Fletch asked.

Jenny nodded. "Yes, and well-dressed, too, unlike her father."

Fletch sat in deep thought, rubbing his chin. "I think what we have here is a father who has sacrificed his needs for his daughter's. He probably doesn't make very much money and recently there has been an acute deterioration of funds for some reason," he said at last.

Jenny thought a moment. "Yes, I think you're right," she said. "What can we do about it?"

He stood to his feet as though to leave. "My church has an organization that furnishes food, clothing, and money to people in need. Say the word and I'll get help immediately." He walked to the door. Jenny knew he meant it.

She followed him across the floor. "That's fantastic," she said. "I'll see what I can find out."

"Well, I better go." He opened the door, then closed it. "I can't remember ever meeting such a caring person before." He opened the door, stepped through, then came back in and closed it again. "And it was terribly nice of you to visit Steve in the hospital." He opened the door once more and stepped through. He closed the door then opened it a crack. "Good night," he called. Then he was gone.

Charley poked her head out of her bedroom door. "Whoa," she said. "That guy could hardly pry himself away from you."

6

Jenny chuckled out loud. Didn't she wish! "Hardly, Charley. He's just super nice."

The next day Jenny asked Annie to stay behind a moment when she dismissed her class for recess. She'd never pump one of her kids, but maybe she could just have a little visit with the girl.

The child approached her desk timidly. Jenny hadn't noticed Annie showing any timidity at all before. She put her arm around Annie's waist. "I enjoyed being with you last night, Annie."

Annie smiled and nodded.

"Was the dinner all right?"

Again the silent nod.

This wasn't getting anywhere and Jenny hated to pry. But there was one thing she just had to know. "Do you mind staying at home alone, Annie?"

Annie's bright eyes grew round. "I never stayed alone until Daddy took you to the movies," she said.

"But I especially invited you too, Annie," Jenny said.

Annie nodded. "I know." She studied Jenny a moment, and giggled. Then she laughed aloud. Her blue eyes sparkled like deep, wind-ruffled water. "My daddy said you were pretty and he wanted to be alone with you."

"Oh." Jenny didn't know how to answer. She didn't want to be responsible for anyone's unhappiness. Not Annie's. Not Vince's.

"I stayed home so he could ask you to be my new mommy, Miss Cornell. Will you?"

All at once Jenny wished she'd gone out for recess. She gathered Annie close and pulled her onto her lap. "Annie," she whispered, "it isn't that simple. It takes a very long time for people to know each other well enough to get married." *Yes?* she asked herself. *How come you're so sure about Fletch? How long have you known him? I'm not sure about Fletch*, she silently replied, *he's just a friend. Barely a friend*, she told herself defiantly.

Annie looked into Jenny's eyes. "I'll stay alone then, Miss Cornell."

That night Jenny told Charley about the failed interrogation attempt. "The worst thing about it," she said, brushing away a tear, "is that she hates being left alone." She sat silent a moment, then continued. "Wouldn't it be fantastic if I could marry her father? We could be a nice little family and live happily ever after." She shook her head. "It could never work. He's really nice, but the chemistry isn't there."

Charley, brusque as usual, put everything into perspective. "You didn't make the problem, Jen, so don't worry about it. What you need to worry about is do they have enough to eat?"

"I checked into Annie's lunches at school today," Jenny said. "She has always been provided free lunches due to her family's low income. So we know she at least gets one decent meal each day."

"Not enough," Charley said. "Want me to go talk to the old man?"

Jenny sighed. She'd love for Charley to do it. "Of course

not," she said. "I'll do it tomorrow after school. Thanks, anyway."

The next day after school Charley finished up the work in the classroom while Jenny drove to Vince's run-down house.

"Well, this is a surprise," he said upon finding Jenny at the door. "Come in, come in." He helped her find a place to sit on the faded couch then sat across from her on a wooden rocker. A smile nearly covered his large face. "To tell you the truth, Jenny," he said, "I thought I'd seen the last of you. I sort of blew it, didn't I?"

Jenny raised her eyebrows and shrugged, smiling. "I think Annie's welfare is the main concern of both of us," she said.

"Yeah? Well, she's top priority with me."

How to pry into a man's private life without upsetting him? She'd make a good try, anyway. "What I'm wondering, Vince," she said carefully, "is—have you had some misfortune recently? Maybe financial misfortune?"

Vince pointed a long wide finger at her. "Hey, the lady's clairvoyant," he said. "Yes, as a matter of fact, we have. I just lost my job at the service station. The guy went bankrupt. He owed me two month's wages, too." He remained silent a moment. Then, "Hey, my Annie didn't go crying to you, did she?"

Jenny shook her head. "Of course not. She's a loyal little girl and you are definitely the king of her universe. I just wondered, from the things I saw. Could you use a little help, Vince? Maybe some groceries, the rent?"

His head fell on his chest, but he jerked it upright almost instantly. "I'd never take anything from you, Jenny. I've heard about teachers' wages. I'm looking hard for something else. We'll make it. The tough part is that now I discover the rat didn't pay his unemployment insurance, so it will take a while to start collecting unemployment checks—if I ever do."

Jenny leaned across and put her hand on his arm. "I didn't mean I would help. Not that I wouldn't like to, but I'm struggling to make ends meet, too. But I talked to an organization that will help you until you're back on your feet. I'll tell them to get in touch, OK?"

Vince slumped in his chair and his face sagged. "I guess. Tell them just for a little while. I've never accepted help in my life."

He filled the doorway as Jenny walked down the rickety steps. "I suppose you don't want anything to do with a person that can't even take care of himself."

Jenny stopped short. "Oh, Vince, that's not it at all." She ran back onto the porch so she could talk directly to him. "I'd love to be your friend and Annie's too, but I should tell you up front that I'm already emotionally involved. It's a one-way street, too," she added wryly.

She picked up Charley at school and hurried home, eager to call Fletch. "He'll accept help, but he's proud," Jenny reported. Then she told him about Vince's job evaporating.

"He'll have help by morning," Fletch said. "Hey! I have another idea. Remember what he said about his mechanical skills? I just may give him a chance to put his ability where his mouth is. If he's really that good, I can use him." He hesitated, then laughed softly. "And you just might get your car fixed," he added.

Wednesday night Charley came home from prayer meeting somewhat subdued. "Adam's really nice," she told Jenny. "But I get the feelin' he's bein' a missionary." She broke into her high volume laugh. "I don't want him to be my missionary, Jen, I want him to like me."

"Are you going to church because you enjoy that or

just to see Adam?" Jenny asked.

"I'm not sure. I enjoy the services a lot. But I love Adam."

"Oh, Charley, you couldn't love him already."

Charley tipped her head and looked at Jenny from the corner of her eyes. "Sure. And look who's talkin'."

"Charley! I've never ever said I love anybody."

"You haven't said you don't, either."

Thursday night Fletch called. "He's had all the help he'll take, Jenny, and I gave him our regular mechanical test. He scored in the top three percent. Know what that means to you? When that time bomb you drive goes off again, we may get to the bottom of it."

"I can hardly wait," Jenny said, grinning. "But say, thanks an awful lot for helping Vince and Annie. I'm coming to really appreciate you—and your church. Give them my thanks, will you?"

Saturday morning Charley knocked on Jenny's bedroom door, then opened it a crack. "Are you awake, Jen?" she whispered.

Jenny had been reading for a while. She laid the book on the nightstand. "Yes, I'm awake," she said to the crack. "Come in."

Charley shoved the door open and burst through. "I wondered if you'd help me fix my face for church this morning," she said. "I do look a little different from the others."

"Gladly." Jenny jumped out of bed, wrapped her blue terrycloth robe around her small body, and pulled out her vanity chair. "Welcome to my salon," she said, using her best French accent and waving grandly toward the chair. "Won't you sit right here while I make you even more beautiful than you already are, though it would seem that were impossible."

Charley barked her harsh laugh and sat.

First, Jenny rubbed a foundation base into Charley's face. "This is called 'cover-up,'" she said. "It blends your skin colors together and hides pimples or blemishes."

"Whoa! Dump it on my freckles, Jen. I'd love for them to disappear," Charley yelled.

"Charley, your freckles are cute," Jenny said, making small circles with a little brush. "They give you character."

Charley grinned. "I know I'm a character, but don't rub it in." After a moment she snapped her fingers. "I mean do rub it in, Jen. Rub it in hard."

Jenny laid the first brush down and picked up another. "Now I'm going to cover the foundation with a thin layer of powder. It will keep the cover-up from shining and also keep it from smearing." She finished that and picked up a much smaller brush. "Now, suck in your cheeks, Charley. I'll give you just a hint of blush to accent your cheek bones."

After a touch of light orange lipstick and a hint of brown eye makeup and mascara, Jenny couldn't believe how pretty Charley looked. The girl's huge green eyes snapped into prominence when her other features were minimized. "You're really a pretty girl, Charley," Jenny said. "I don't blame Adam for wanting to take you out."

Then she used the curling brush on Charley's long hair and in a little while the coppery mop settled into a soft frame for her lovely new face.

"Hey, I like that," Charley said when Jenny turned her to the mirror. "Maybe I'll go after Fletch, now." She looked up at Jenny. "Just kidding, Jen. Anyway, he doesn't compare with Adam. You'll see. If I ever get him into the house."

Jenny could hardly wait for Charley to return from church. Surely Adam would appreciate her new look.

Finally, 12:15 came and the door opened quietly, which was not like Charley. "Jen, where are you?" she called.

Jenny tossed her magazine onto the coffee table. "Right here," she called. "How'd he like it?" She hurried into the kitchen to find a dark-haired young man standing beside the door. Charley towered over him more than the two inches she'd admitted to.

"Oops. Sorry, I didn't know you had company," Jenny said, backing out of the kitchen.

Charley rushed through the doorway, grabbed Jenny's arm, and pulled her back. "Jenny, I want you to meet my friend, Adam Stanwick. Adam, my reluctant roommate."

Adam took two large strides toward Jenny and extended his hand. "I'm glad to meet you at last, Jenny. I've been hearing a lot about you. All good, of course."

"Don't listen to my roommate, Adam," Jenny said, rolling her eyes to the ceiling. "She's just so thankful for a roof over her head."

He shook his head. His white teeth glistened beneath his mustache and his black eyes sparkled with mysterious thoughts. "Oh, she isn't the one talking about you." He glanced at Charley. "Well, she mentions you once in a while—not more than every other sentence, though."

"Could you stay for lunch, Adam?" Jenny asked, hesitantly.

"Thanks, but I couldn't," he said. "My folks are expecting me. We're taking a long hike in the Blues this afternoon."

Jenny put the roast into the oven while Charley walked to the car with Adam. "Well?" she asked when Charley burst through the back door in her normal way.

Charley spun in a circle, then held her arms up and out, like a model. "He told me I look pretty, Jen. But he could have invited me to go hiking in the Blues. I think I'm a soul to save. Period."

"Maybe. You'll just have to wait and hope, like I do with Fletch. Now, how about making a salad to go with the fantastic meal I'm preparing?"

After lunch Charley brought out a pile of leaflets. "Adam gave me these, Jen," she said. "Want to look at them? He said they tell about his church."

"What do I care about his church?" Jenny asked, reaching for the top one. She ended up spending the afternoon reading through them. She found them interesting and easy to agree with until she came to the one proclaiming Saturday to be the Sabbath. She read the entire leaflet, which showed the Sabbath was created on the seventh day of creation week, Jesus kept the Sabbath, and His disciples kept it after He ascended to heaven.

"How could they possibly know which day is which?" she asked Charley. "Creation happened a long time ago and history wasn't recorded for many years."

Charley shrugged. "I wouldn't know. Far as that goes, it doesn't matter much to me. Most of this stuff is just like I learned in my church."

The girls didn't discuss the subject further, but as Jenny read the rest of the leaflets she wondered how the Seventh-day Adventists could be sure which day was the ancient Sabbath.

Monday afternoon the teachers assembled in the teachers' lounge as usual, visiting and gossiping. "I have a trivia question for a historian," Jenny said when the conversation lagged.

Several of the men accepted the challenge so Jenny continued. "Do you know how long the weekly cycle has been undisturbed? In other words I need to know how far back we can be sure the days of the week have been exactly as they are now."

"Not very long," one of the teachers said. "I think the calendar has been changed several times in the past few centuries."

"The calendar has been changed but the weekly cycle has never been interrupted," Martin Mandell said importantly.

"I know how you can find out, if it's important," Mr. Brock said. "Write to the U.S. Naval Observatory in Washington, D.C. They'll know."

The talk drifted to other topics but Jenny tucked that address into her mental notebook and later wrote her question to them, including a self-addressed stamped envelope.

That night Jenny's mother called and asked her to bring Charley for dinner Sunday evening. "I'm afraid to, Mom," Jenny said. "My car still quits whenever it feels like it." Jenny told her about Fletch and how he went for a ride with her, hoping it would act up.

"Bring him too, dear. We'd love to have him."

Jenny's heart grew too large for her chest. How would it look, asking him to meet her family?

"Why the silence, Jenny?" Mom asked. "Don't you like the man?"

Did she *like* the man? If Mom only knew how much she liked him.

"He's OK, Mom," she said, trying to sound indifferent. "But I'm not sure I'm brave enough to ask him to come. He's a busy person."

"Does he have a family? I suppose he would want to be with them on the weekend."

"He's not married." Mom would get the whole story out of her yet.

"Oh?" Mom put a light-hearted lift in her voice. "How old is this super mechanic, anyway?"

"I don't know, about 24, I think. His age and marital status don't matter, Mom. I just think he doesn't want to waste a whole afternoon and evening. He works all week, you know."

"I know. You ask him."

After she hung up, Jenny asked Charley to go, but she had some kind of plans for that day. "Call Fletch," Charley insisted. "You'll soon find out if he wants to go."

Jenny dialed the number with her heart in her throat. Maybe Fletch wouldn't be home. But he answered the phone. "Do you think it would be safe for me to drive to LaGrande next Sunday?" she asked, unable to bring herself to ask outright.

"Don't count on it." His rich voice sent goose bumps charging up her spine. "Do you really have to go?"

Now was the time. "No, but my mother thinks I do, if you get my drift."

He laughed. "I get it." The silence almost became embarrassing before he continued. "Would you like some company?"

Jenny couldn't believe how easy that had turned out to be. "That's a fantastic idea. I'd feel a lot better with a mechanic along."

"OK, Vince's turning out to be a great worker and really knowledgeable about cars. He might just be the one who could locate the problem. Would you like to take him and his little girl?"

Oh, no! What could she say now? If she said she didn't want Vince, Fletch would know she wanted him. And Vince would get ideas if she took him along. Besides, an afternoon with Fletch had sounded so wonderful. She felt herself wilting. Maybe she'd just stay home. How did she get herself into these messes anyway?

"Or I could go if that would simplify things for you," Fletch added softly after the silence became embarrassingly long.

Jenny nodded and pushed the receiver against her ear. "That would simplify things, all right. If you're sure you have time. I don't want to be a pest."

Fletch laughed. "I owe you, Jenny. You've been a pretty good sport about that lemon we sold you."

Jenny thanked him and they set the time. After she hung up she went to bed depressed. He owed her! Why couldn't he have said he'd love to go anywhere with her? Anytime! She could truthfully say that to him, but of course she wouldn't.

Saturday morning Jenny fixed Charley's hair and makeup for church again. Physically tamed, her personality almost seemed quieter, too. Jenny knew this could only be to Charley's advantage in her quest for Adam. But Charley came home from church more discouraged than the previous week.

Sunday afternoon finally came and Jenny fixed herself as carefully as she had Charley. She examined her reflection in the steamy mirror after her shower. Nice straight nose, full pink lips, high cheekbones. She looked into the monstrous blue eyes. She knew her eyes and dark lashes were her best feature, but the rest of her didn't look so bad, either. Why couldn't Fletch notice? She reached for the curling brush. Her hair would be perfect today. It brushed out soft and feathered back perfectly. The ends curled just a little. Just right.

Fletch arrived on time. He automatically put Jenny in the passenger seat and ran behind the car to the driver's side. "Set for a nice afternoon?" he asked, fastening his shoulder harness.

"I'm trying." She managed a smile. "I hope I didn't take you away from something important."

He backed slowly into the street and started down the hill. "I didn't have a thing planned. I'm glad to help," he said. "Now, are we hoping for this thing to quit on us or to run like a brush fire?"

"I don't know," she said honestly. "I guess we're hoping for it to quit. I can't keep pestering you forever."

He put his dimples on duty with a wide smile. "Sure you can."

Jenny's hand flew to her chest to quiet her wild heart. He said she could bother him forever! He must have some feelings for her!

"After all," he continued, "I get a nice ride and a free meal, don't I?"

Oof. The balloon popped.

"Of course," she said.

They rode quietly for a while, enjoying the rolling farmland beside the freeway. "I really like your car," Fletch said. When Jenny didn't respond he continued. "Vince has worked for me only a couple of weeks and he's already my top mechanic. I don't understand why he worked at a service station for minimum wages. Things are looking better for him and his little Annie."

"Do you spend your whole life doing nice things for other people?" Jenny asked, carefully watching the grain fields.

The quick motion of his head turning toward her caused Jenny to face him. "No, as a matter of fact, I don't," he said. "I spend most of my time doing nice things for me—like today."

Jenny said nothing, waiting for the follow-up that would bash her to the ground. None came.

In seemingly no time at all, they turned into Jenny's

family's driveway. The front door opened and Mom and Dad ran down the front steps. Dad opened Jenny's door and she tumbled into his arms. "Hi, Dad," she said into his neck, "I'm so glad to be here."

Dad looked over Jenny's head at Fletch coming around the car with his hand extended. Dad squeezed Jenny tightly and extended his hand to Fletch. Then Jenny saw the telltale twinkle in his blue eyes. "Young man," he said, "I'll bet my last dollar you wish she were in your arms instead of mine."

7

Jenny jerked away from her father. "Dad!" she whispered, "he's only the mechanic trying to find what's wrong with my car."

Dad's sparkling eyes traveled over Fletch, starting at his neatly combed brown hair, through his soft brown eyes, to his curved firm mouth and square chin. Then they took in the younger man's broad shoulders in his light blue knit shirt and jeans. Finally Dad's mischievous eyes returned to Jenny's and he ruffled her perfectly arranged hair. "Sure, he's just the mechanic. Don't try to fool your old dad, baby."

Jenny turned her red face to Fletch and shrugged. Then her laughter joined Dad's. "I have no idea what he's blathering about," she said, trudging toward the porch. "Come on, let's go in."

Dinner turned out better than Jenny dared to expect after the shaky beginning. Dad and Fletch played chess while Jenny helped Mom with the dishes. "He's awfully nice, dear," Mom said, squirting lotion on her hands. She raised her blue eyes to Jenny and arched her still-dark eyebrows. "And so good-looking. I wouldn't mind if he were more than your mechanic."

Jenny held out her hands for lotion, then rubbed them

together thoughtfully. She wouldn't mind, either, but—.
"He isn't, though, Mom," she said cheerfully. "He's just trying desperately to fix my car." They went into the living room where the men were playing.

"Checkmate," Fletch said, looking quizzically at Jenny. He stood, walked to her chair, and plopped down on the ottoman, facing her. "Think we should go home?" he asked. "It'll be dark before we get there now, and I forgot to bring a flashlight." He shook his head, and the curl fell over his forehead again.

Dad heisted his round body from the chair and left the room, returning a moment later with a five-cell flashlight. "Here, Fletch. The batteries are new and it's as bright as an electric light bulb."

Fletch gladly accepted the light and the folks walked to the car with them. Fletch put Jenny in, then started around the car.

"Hey!" Dad bellowed. "How about coming for Thanksgiving dinner, young man? My wife cooks a mean turkey."

Fletch shook Dad's hand again. "Thanks, Mr. Cornell. I'd really love to, but we have a big family thing at my house."

"I'll be here, Dad," Jenny called as Fletch eased the car from the driveway.

Fletch rolled up his window. "I really like your folks, Jenny. But does your dad always act like you're a desperate old maid?"

Jenny laughed. "No, this is the first time, but he always finds something to persecute me about." After a pause she continued, "I guess this is the first time I've brought anyone home. Maybe he thinks I am desperate." They rode silently for several miles. "On the other hand," Jenny continued as though there hadn't been a break in the conversation, "I've been away from home only three months."

"Maybe your dad doesn't like you out in the big world alone," Fletch mused. "Did you live at home during your college years?"

"Sure did. Even then I had to take out loans. I'm paying them back now. I'm not finding it very easy, either." She rifled through her purse for gum and offered it to him.

He took a stick, unwrapped it and stuck it into his mouth. "What about you, Fletch," she continued, "didn't you ever wish to go to college?"

His mouth dropped a tiny bit. "Sure. I graduated from Walla Walla College two years ago last spring."

"I'm shocked," Jenny admitted. "I don't know why, but it never occurred to me. What did you major in, auto mechanics?"

He laughed. "Not exactly, although I took a one-year mechanical technology course. I ended up with two degrees, Jenny, business administration and theology."

"Wow, I'm impressed. How long did it take you?"

"You really didn't have to ask that." His eyes twinkled. "It took five years. I thought I could do it in four, but it didn't work out."

"But you got three educations. Do you plan to continue working at Ford indefinitely?"

"Only for a while. After graduating from Walla Walla I went to Andrews University in Michigan to work on my Master's degree. My father became seriously ill so I came home to help out at the garage. He's much better now, so I'll be going back soon." He glanced at her then back at the road. "When I finish school I'll go into the ministry."

"You'll make a fantastic minister, Fletch," she blurted without thinking. "You're so nice and kind and good." She leaned back, her face hot and her stomach rolling uncontrollably at her forwardness.

He flushed too, then said, "Thank you, Jenny. You made my day. I have to be a minister because serving my Lord is the most important thing in my life."

They rode in comfortable silence most of the way home.

"I seem to see the exit ahead," Fletch finally said. "The flighty little Mustang behaved like a thoroughbred today. Maybe we're getting it trained."

Fifteen minutes later Fletch turned off the switch and handed Jenny the key. He climbed out of the Mustang and walked with her to the porch. He leaned against the door. "Thanks for the really nice day," he said. "I can't tell you how much I enjoyed it."

"Thanks for coming. I wouldn't have dared go alone."

"Well, I suppose I should be going," he said. "Oh, how is Annie now? She has good lunches, doesn't she?"

"She has hot lunches so I don't worry about them."

He started down the steps. "OK. I just wanted to be sure. Well, thanks again for the nice day." He took two steps on the sidewalk, turned, and ran up beside Jenny again. "How are Charley and Adam doing?" he asked, looking down at her. His eyes shone like a dozen stars.

"I'm really not sure." Jenny could hardly concentrate enough to make sensible answers.

"OK, just wondered." He ran down the steps, turned, and said, " 'Bye, Jenny. Thanks a lot." He didn't even take one step on the sidewalk that time until he bounded back. "What do you . . . ? Oh, forget it, I have to go. 'Bye." He ran to his car and tore off down the street.

What was that all about? Jenny wondered as she let herself in.

Later, Jenny sat on her vanity chair and brushed her

hair into a soft dark cloud. She wouldn't hold her breath until he called. Somehow she knew he wouldn't. Oh, but she wished he would. She had never known such a kind loving person in her life. And those dimples!

A week later Jenny received an answer from the U.S. Naval Observatory telling her the weekly cycle had been consistent since the time of Christ. Well, that would make Saturday the Sabbath, all right. She had to give Christ credit for knowing which day was the Sabbath. She decided she must learn more about this intriguing subject.

The next afternoon she stopped at the Christian Supply Store and on the advice of the clerk bought a New International Version of the Bible. She planned to find out for herself what the Bible had to say about the Sabbath—and everything else.

"What ya readin' Jen?" Charley asked when she came in one night.

Jenny held it up so Charley could see the front.

"A Bible? I don't believe it. What are you tryin' to do, make points with Fletch?" She laughed, not quite so loudly as she used to.

Jenny sighed and laid the Bible on the end table. "Charley, when are you going to get it into your head that Fletch isn't interested in me?" she asked quietly. "I'm reading it out of curiosity about the Sabbath. It probably wouldn't hurt you a whole lot to do a little reading. After all, you're going to that church."

Charley laughed. "I read enough Bible and learned enough verses to last a lifetime, Jen." She went to her room.

One Wednesday night Jenny let Adam in and went looking for Charley. She knocked quietly on the girl's bedroom door and entered at Charley's invitation. "Adam's here, Charley. Are you ready?" When she got a good look,

Jenny knew Charley lacked a lot of being ready. She lay on her bed in her pajamas and robe, wearing no makeup at all.

"What's going on?" Jenny asked. "Why aren't you ready?"

Charley, lying on her stomach across her bed, glanced up from her magazine and back down as though it were all-absorbing. "Tell him I'm not goin', Jen."

"I will not!" Jenny roared. "The least you can do is tell him yourself. Why didn't you call?"

Charley studied her magazine with intense interest. "Tell him, Jen, or have a nice evenin' with him. I'm not goin' out there."

Jenny marched back to the living room, terribly angry at her roommate. She should just take Adam right into Charley's room!

Adam stood when Jenny entered the room. She tried to smile at him. "I'm sorry, Adam, I guess she's not going," she said, attempting a casualness she didn't feel.

Adam's expression didn't change. "Well, I guess I better go, then." He stepped toward the kitchen door, then turned to Jenny. "How about you, kiddo?" He smiled and Jenny understood Charley's feelings. The guy had a sincere, friendly smile. "Why don't you come and see what we're all about, Jenny?" he asked softly.

Jenny felt sorely tempted. Fletch would almost certainly be there and just a glimpse of him would make her happy. Or would it? She shook her head. If and when the time came that she went to church it would never be to see a man. "I'm sorry, but I have a big evening here," she said.

As soon as she heard the car leave, Jenny slammed into Charley's room without knocking. "What do you think you're doing?" she yelled, sparks flying from her blue eyes.

Charley raised her eyes from her magazine. "Readin',"

she answered calmly and dropped her eyes.

Jenny snatched the magazine and hurled it into a corner of the room. She dropped onto the edge of the bed. "Don't you think that was a little rude? Even for you?" she shouted.

"Whoa!" Charley said, a wide smile lighting her freckled face. "That was good, Jen. I didn't think you had that much fire in you. With a little more practice you could be a real person."

Jenny couldn't stay mad at her incorrigible roommate. "All right, Charley," she said, returning the smile. "What's going on?"

Charley pulled herself to a sitting position in the middle of the bed, her legs crossed Indian fashion in front of her. "What's goin' on? Nothin', Jen. That's the trouble. I refuse to be a missionary project. He never cared a fig for me. He was just looking for souls." A moment later she smiled. "I guess that's a pretty good thing to do," she admitted grudgingly, "but I wanted something else."

"Oh." Jenny took in a big breath. "Well, don't you think you should have let him know? And what am I supposed to do next time?"

Charley grinned impudently. "I don't know, roommate. That's your problem. I'll probably be out."

Jenny returned to her Bible reading. She spent several hours reading every night, while Charley disappeared on her cycle. To Jenny's surprise she found the Bible intriguing and she began to feel she knew Jesus a little. She learned that Fletch's kind loving ways were patterned after Jesus. She also learned that Jesus loved the Sabbath and nowhere in the gospels did He mention its demise.

One morning in late November Jenny pulled her drapes to find a thick blanket of snow covering the city. Snow clung to the trees and bushes around her apartment, making an early Christmas card for her to enjoy.

She pounded on Charley's door. "Come quick, Charley," she called, "and see what God did while we slept."

Charley poked a sleepy face into the kitchen a few minutes later, a crooked smile wandering over her features. "I must really have been asleep," she said. "I thought I heard you out here ranting about God."

Jenny thought back. She had! She had unconsciously spoken of God as though it were perfectly natural for her. "I did, didn't I?" she said happily. She turned Charley to face the window wall.

"Hey, that's neat," Charley said as she looked over the city. "Yesterday the buildings were all different colored and some were much fancier than others. Some were just plain shabby. This morning everything looks pure and white, and equally beautifully."

"Charley!" Jenny almost shouted. "It just hit me. That's how it is with God. People are all different colored, some shabby, some beautiful, but when God's righteousness covers us we're all the same color and equally beautiful. Isn't that fantastic?"

The clamor of the telephone interrupted.

"It snowed last night," Fletch said in Jenny's ear.

"Yes, isn't it beautiful?" Jenny asked. "All the dirty and messy things are hidden—just as if they weren't there."

Fletch remained silent a moment. "You know, Jenny, that is what our Lord does for us. He covers our sins as though they weren't there. But unlike the snow, which melts and reveals the dirt again, when we accept Him as our Saviour, our sins are gone forever."

What a gorgeous way to put it. Jenny remained silent, enjoying the beautiful thought.

"Well," Fletch finally said, sounding subdued, "I just called to remind you to put some snow tires on your car.

That hill could be a mess to climb in icy weather."

Jenny broke into a happy smile. "Well, thanks, Fletch. How nice of you to think of me. Could you do that?"

"No, we don't sell tires," he said. "I think the best place for you would be out by your school at the intersection of highway 395 and Southgate Place. Les Schwaub and Goodyear have stores there."

Charley, who had been riding her motorcycle to school, gladly rode in the little Mustang that morning. As Jenny eased her car down the hill on King Avenue, she marveled at Fletch's thoughtfulness.

After school she had snow tires put on and the little Mustang galloped up the icy hill with no effort.

While the girls cleared away the supper dishes Charley said, "You should have told Fletch to tell Adam I'm not going to church anymore."

Jenny dropped a plate into its slot in the dishwasher, then straightened up. "No, I shouldn't have, Charley," she said, her hands planted firmly on her slim hips. "You should have the decency to call Adam—the guy you're in love with, I might add—and tell him yourself." She picked up two glasses, rinsed them, and dropped them into the top rack.

"Jen," Charley said, "once in love isn't necessarily always in love, you know."

"No, I didn't know," Jenny said. "I thought I was doomed to spend the rest of my life in love with a man who is only interested in helping me."

Charley gave the counter a swipe with the cloth and the girls raced to the living room. Jenny sat on the couch and Charley turned the TV on.

She sat down and continued the conversation. "One of these days you'll wake up, shake your head, and say, 'Fletch? Fletch who?'"

Jenny, who had already opened her Bible, looked up. "How come it still hurts so much then?" she asked.

"Because you aren't over it . . ." Charley's program began and she forgot what she'd started to say.

Jenny took her Bible and went to bed.

"I'm not so sure I like the snow after all, Jen," Charley said the next morning as the girls ate breakfast. They had carried their plates into the living room to enjoy the lovely view while they ate.

"Oh, Charley," Jenny sighed, taking in the winter beauty spread before them. "What's not to enjoy?"

"I'm grounded. At least I'm smart enough to leave my bike in the garage at night."

Jenny thoughtfully chewed a bite of toast. She'd been wondering where Charley had spent her evenings lately. She swallowed. "Where do you need to go that's so important?" she asked.

Charley shook her red brush pile mysteriously. "I'll never tell. I may have a big romance sizzling, for all you know."

Charley didn't even take her cycle out in the daytime during that icy spell, but within a week the sun melted the snow and left a muddy wet world for the girls to view from their perch on the hillside.

"Let's just open a can of soup tonight," Charley urged on the first night the snow was gone.

"But I'm hungry," Jenny said.

"OK, two cans." Charley had two cans out of the cupboard before Jenny could answer. She opened them and dumped them into a pan, then rinsed each can with water and poured that in, too.

Charley put two bowls on the table, then crackers. "Want a sandwich?" she asked. Without waiting for an answer she pulled the cheese and mayonnaise from the refrigerator.

Finally Jenny caught on. "Hey, what's the hurry?" she asked, laughing. "Going somewhere?"

Charley sprayed Pam into the skillet, dropped a cheese sandwich in, then looked up and smiled. "You got it, roomie. In ten minutes I'm out of here."

Jenny spent the evening reading the four Gospels again. She kept so busy that Charley returned before she became lonely.

Jenny read the Gospels twice a week, and other parts of the Bible between times. She began to fall in love with the Lord Jesus, who had loved her enough to die for her before she even knew Him. One night she picked up the phone and called the pastor of the Seventh-day Adventist church. After telling him what she was doing she asked, "Can you give me any better suggestions for Bible study?"

"You're doing a fantastic job," he said. "I wish I could get my congregation to read half as much Bible." After a moment he continued, "I'd like to visit you, Miss Cornell."

Charley's jeering face flashed into Jenny's mind. She didn't need that. But Charley was gone most evenings. And she would like to talk to the man and learn more about his church. "I think it would be all right," she said. "Could you come around 7:30 on a week night?"

They agreed on the next evening and Jenny returned to her studying.

The next morning the phone rang as the girls stepped through the kitchen door. Charley shrugged. "I don't hear anything, do you?" she asked, closing the door.

"I better get it," Jenny said. "It might be important."

"May I speak to Charley?" a male voice asked.

As she waited for Charley to finish the conversation, Jenny tried to think who the caller was. *I've heard that voice before*, she thought. *I know I have.*

Charley returned and the girls ran to the car. "Who called?" Jenny asked as she backed out of the garage.

Charley looked mysterious again. "Oh, just a friend. You probably don't even know him."

"But I do," Jenny insisted. The conversation returned to Jenny's mind several times that day. It bothered her that she couldn't place the voice.

That evening Jenny hurried with supper, eager to get Charley away before the minister came. Charley appeared relaxed and started to help load the dishwasher.

Jenny pushed her from the kitchen. "You go on, Charley," she said. "I don't mind cleaning the kitchen."

"No problem, Jen," Charley said, returning to her place by the dishwasher. "Let me do the dishes tonight. It's my turn and I'm not goin' anywhere, anyway."

8

What! What about the minister coming? Charley always went out at night. "How come you're staying here?" Jenny asked, trying to cover her surprise.

"Because I live here," Charley said, grinning. "Do you mind?"

All of a sudden it hit Jenny. The morning telephone call! She felt sure she recognized that voice. Who was it, anyway? "Of course I don't mind, Charley," Jenny said. "It was the telephone call, wasn't it? He told you not to come."

Charley nodded. "You guessed it, Jen."

She had to try once more. "I'm sure I recognized the voice, Charley. Who was it?"

Charley shook her wild red head. "Nope. You wouldn't know him in a million years." She chuckled. "Not from me, anyway."

Jenny went to brush her teeth and try to figure what to do about tonight. Maybe Charley would go to bed early. Before 7:30? Jenny showered, put on fresh makeup, brushed her hair, and returned to the living room half an hour later, dressed in fresh white slacks. A red tie brightened her white blouse.

Charley glanced up from the TV and raised her eyebrows. "What's this?" she asked loudly. "I suppose you've been runnin' off every night as soon as I'm out of sight."

Jenny sat down beside her roommate, still not knowing how to tell her a minister was coming. "I'm not going anywhere," she said quietly, "but I'm having company in a little while."

"Aha," Charley jumped to her feet. "And you want me out of here."

"Sit down," Jenny said, patting the still-warm couch beside her. After Charley sat, Jenny continued. "Of course, I don't want you to leave, but could you stay in your bedroom? He won't be here long."

Charley flipped the TV off and returned to the couch. "It's not Fletch, is it?" she asked.

Jenny shook her head.

"And it is a guy, didn't you say?" Charley asked.

Jenny nodded, feeling guilty. How could she call a minister a guy?

"Great!" Charley said, hugging Jenny. "You've been mooning for that jerk long enough. I'm in my bedroom already. See?" she added, "I told you you'd get over Fletch, didn't I?"

Don't I wish! Jenny thought as Charley's door shut with a crash.

Jenny ushered her guest through the kitchen into the living room and took his overcoat. She couldn't believe how young he was. He stood before the open drapes, drinking in the lights of Pendleton. "What a gorgeous view," he said, extending his hand to Jenny. "I'm Bailey Miller, from the Seventh-day Adventist church."

Jenny took his hand. "And I'm Jenny Cornell, from McKay Creek School," she responded, chuckling softly. "May I get you something?"

He settled into the orange overstuffed chair. "No thanks, I'm comfortable," he said. Then his gray eyes met

Jenny's. "Do you belong to a church?"

"No, I've just started reading the Bible. I'd like to know more about your church."

The bedroom door burst open and Charley stood in the center of the living room. "Pastor Miller! What are you doing here?"

The minister stood up and shook hands with Charley. "Just visiting," he said, smiling. "How are things with you?"

Charley turned to Jenny with a loud laugh. "What a trick, Jen. You're the girl who doesn't like religion and here you are, after your second Seventh-day Adventist. No wonder you wanted me out of sight."

Hot streaks raced up Jenny's cheeks, until her whole face burned. Tears bubbled into her eyes. Why did Charley do this to her, anyway?

"I just dropped by to see how Miss Cornell was coming on her Bible reading," the man said. "Would you care to join our study?"

Charley gave Jenny a strange look and disappeared into her room.

The minister sat down. "Don't feel bad, Miss Cornell," he said kindly. "We all understand Charley. She attended our church a few times, you know."

Jenny sat down, too. "Call me Jenny," she said, "and I'm not after you. Please believe me. And I haven't been after any other man either, let alone a Seventh-day Adventist. I'm not like that."

"I know, Jenny," he said softly. "I could tell right away that you aren't. And everyone calls me Bailey." He picked up his Bible and started talking as though Charley's interruption hadn't happened.

Jenny still felt angry at Charley when she got up the next morning. "Why did you do that to me last night?" she asked when Charley slid into her place at the breakfast table.

"Why did you do that to me?" Charley returned. "You could have told me it was a minister. Then I wouldn't have been so surprised when I heard him talking." She reached for the milk and poured it over her oatmeal. Then she looked up at Jenny and smiled. "He's a fantastic guy, Jen. Hey, why don't you go hear him preach sometime?"

"After your performance I'll probably never see him again," Jenny said ruefully. "And I'm not the least bit interested in him, Charley. Really I'm not."

Charley dumped her toast crust into her oatmeal dish and stood up. "Your loss, Jen. I wish you were."

That night Jenny had just fallen asleep when the roar of the big cycle awakened her. Then the sound of doors slamming brought her tumbling from her bed and into the living room.

"Hey, I hoped you'd still be up," Charley said grinning. She pointed to the couch. "Sit." Jenny sat. Charley strode toward the kitchen. "Don't go away," she said, speaking over her shoulder.

What's going on? Jenny wondered.

Charley came in carrying a tray filled with steaming cups of chocolate and set it on the coffee table. She handed one to Jenny and took the other herself. She settled on the rocker and her green eyes met Jenny's. "Think you'd like to have the place to yourself?" she asked, almost in a whisper.

"What?" Jenny jumped to her feet, sloshing chocolate into her saucer. "No, I don't want the place to myself, Charley. What are you talking about?" She sat back down, feeling as though Charley had kicked her in the stomach.

Charley grinned lazily into Jenny's eyes. "Well, after

last night, I thought I might take this guy up on his offer to live with him."

Jenny reached for Charley's hand. "Don't do it, Charley," she pleaded. "I want you here with me, but more than that, you'd hate yourself. Remember your religious upbringing. You know, the one that clings like lint?"

Charley retrieved her hand and sat quietly a moment. Then she nodded. "It really does. Sometimes I wish I could wash all those memories away."

Jenny shook her head, feeling better. "You don't want to wash them away. They mean a lot to you and will mean even more one of these days." Jenny relaxed, realizing Charlie wouldn't leave her. That must have been her way of saying she was sorry. "Well, that's settled. Should we go to bed?" she asked, getting up.

The next morning Charley roared off down the hill earlier than usual. Jenny suspected she went to tell the man she wouldn't move in with him. As Jenny put the last touches of makeup on, the phone rang. It was Bailey Miller, the minister. "I'd like to study with you on a regular basis," he said. "You've come along so well on your own, but I'm sure I can fill in some of the cracks. Would it be all right for me to come there, now that your roommate understands what's going on?"

"Sure, why not?" Jenny said. "She can't do any worse than she did last time."

The young minister hesitated a moment, then, "Do you think it would help if I brought my wife?"

Jenny's heart leaped. "Yes! That would be wonderful. Please bring her." They came on Monday evenings and Charley managed to be gone on the first occasion as well as most of the others.

One evening Charley roared home from school on her bike, and ran breathlessly into the house. "Do I ever have something to show you!" she yelled, throwing her coat onto the living room carpet. "Let's eat so we can go."

Jenny, doubtful, said, "You tell me what it is, first."

Charley threw herself into a chair. "Oh, Jen," she wailed, "why can't you ever do anything spontaneous, just to be doin' it? All right, if you want to ruin the surprise I'll tell you." Her eyes looked almost angry, but she continued, "I have a neat house to show you."

"OK," Jenny said, feeling properly ashamed of herself. "Let's go before supper while it's still light."

"All right!" Charley jumped up and slapped Jenny on the back. "You're improvin'."

As they drove down the hill on King Avenue Jenny wondered where this house would be. She didn't have to wait long. "Turn here," Charley commanded, pointing left. Jenny turned. Charley directed her until they drove east on Furnish Street.

"Slow down, it's right across this intersection," Charley instructed. "Now, park. Right here." Jenny parked, turned off the ignition, and looked at the house Charley pointed at.

"Wow!" Jenny said. The ivory-colored house stood three stories high. A large shady porch wrapped around the house and four creamy columns supported the steep shingled roof. Many wide wooden steps led from the sidewalk to the porch, where two wide swings swayed gently in the breeze. Narrow lap-siding and many-paned wooden windows gave the house an old but elegant look.

Charley leaned forward to see past Jenny. "Is that a house or what?" she asked, her green eyes sparkling happily.

"It looks really old," Jenny said, still taking it all in, "but it's truly beautiful." She turned to face Charley. "But why did I have to see this particular house?" Jenny laughed. "I know. You want to buy it."

Charley shook her head. "That house isn't for sale. It belongs to a friend of yours, Jen. Guess who lives there?"

Jenny looked at it some more. "You may as well tell me, Charley. I don't know many people in this town."

Charley laughed loudly and poked Jenny on the arm. "Your true love lives there, Jen." She leaned back and laughed some more.

"Fletch? Fletch lives in that house?" Jenny couldn't believe her ears. "Are you sure? Charley! Fletch lives in that house? Fletch lives in that house and we've been sitting here in this red Mustang gawking at it? How could you do this to me, Charley? He's probably sitting inside watching us sitting outside ogling his house." Jenny shoved the key into the ignition. "We're getting out of here," she snapped.

But when she turned the key the car didn't start. After a moment of grinding the starter Jenny lifted horrified eyes to Charley. "I'm going to be sick," she whispered.

Charley's freckles stood out against her white face. "I'm sorry, Jen," she whispered. "I didn't think." She pushed a sleeve up and glanced at her watch. "I don't think he's home, yet. Maybe it'll start in a few minutes."

"When has it ever started in a few minutes?" Jenny asked, climbing out. She walked quickly down the block with Charley following a few steps behind. She turned the corner and walked into an alley.

"Wait, Jen, where are you going?" Charley called.

Jenny stopped and leaned against a power pole. "I had to find a place to be sick," she answered quietly as Charley caught up. "But I think I feel better now." The cool air felt good against her hot cheeks. "I can't go back and face Fletch, Charley," she said.

"Well," Charley drawled, "since it's my fault we're here, I guess you could catch a bus home. I'll face him."

"Good idea. Actually this isn't very far from our apartment. It might feel good to walk." Jenny turned and walked back in the direction of the car—and Fletch's house—and the apartment.

As Jenny walked she thought about Charley. For sure she'd tell Fletch that Jenny had been there. And ran away.

"I guess I may as well stay and face him, Charley," Jenny said when they reached the Mustang.

"I thought so," Charley said. "It's worth the shame to see him again, isn't it?"

"Maybe so, Charley. Maybe so."

They climbed back into the Mustang to talk strategy. "Just go knock on the door and ask for him," Charley suggested.

"No way," Jenny said. "You go. Nothing scares you."

As they argued, a brown car pulled in behind them and Fletch ran to Jenny's door. "Hi, Jenny," he said enthusiastically. "What a nice surprise. What are you doing in this part of town?"

"I thought I'd just bring the car to you this time and make it handy," she said, laughing. A moment later she discovered she couldn't stop laughing. Then tears burst all over her face.

He opened the door and pulled her to him, patting her gently. "I'm so sorry about this lemon, Jenny," he murmured, still patting and squeezing. A few minutes later he pushed her away from him and wiped her tears with a tissue. Then he nodded his head. "We'll get it fixed. Maybe this time. I'll call Vince and we'll go over it together." He took her face in his hands and looked into her eyes. "We should do it right away, before it gets dark. Are you all right?"

Jenny nodded.

He shut the door, smiled a friendly smile, then waved and ran across the street.

"Whoa!" Charley bellowed. "Somethin's goin' on here."

Jenny sniffed. "No, it isn't," she choked. "He's just nice." She sniffled some more. "And he feels badly about the car."

One minute later Fletch ran down the steps and back to the car. Jenny rolled down the window. "He's on his way. This may be it, Jenny. I'm glad the car hasn't been moved."

"Thanks, Fletch," Jenny stammered. "I'm sorry to be such a pain."

Vince drove up, parked his old pickup in front of the Mustang, and hopped out. Annie climbed out, too. The men met and began talking.

Jenny stepped out of the car and called Annie. The little girl came running and Jenny pulled her seat forward so Annie could climb in. "How are you tonight, Annie?" she asked, attempting a big smile.

Annie scooted close to Charley and smiled at Jenny. "I'm fine, Miss Cornell," she said. "Is your car broken?"

The men had raised the hood and Jenny wanted to watch. "It sure is," she said idly. "Could you stay with Miss Haywood, Annie?"

Charley put her arm around Annie and the little girl snuggled against her. "She's fine," Charley said. "Go do what you have to."

Jenny leaned over to watch. "I think it needs a new condenser," Vince said, wiggling something.

Fletch's hands flew all over, feeling this, jiggling that. "Not the condenser, Vince," he answered. "I checked that last time it was in." Vince worked awhile then said, "How about the ignition switch?"

His voice, Jenny thought. What is it about Vince's voice?

"Nope. Checked that, too," Fletch said quietly.

The men worked silently for several minutes, then Fletch let out a yell Jenny didn't think him capable of. "I have it! It's right here! Vince, get a feel of this!"

A moment later Vince's face brightened, too. "You're right," he said. "It's broken clean in two."

Fletch turned to Jenny, his eyes gleaming. "We got it, little one. Want to see? I can show you without getting you greasy." Holding her hand in his, he placed her thumb and forefinger around an electric cable until she felt a break inside. She looked into his eyes, nodding.

"The plastic insulation on the outside held it together until something bumped it apart," he explained. "Then slamming the hood down or some other bump lined it up again."

Vince looked at Fletch with admiration in his eyes. "I'd never have found it," he said.

Fletch grinned his happiness. "I'll bet we don't have one of those cables with us, do we?" he asked.

Vince shook his head slowly. "Want me to go get one?"

"Sure," Fletch said. Then, "No, why don't we haul it in and give it a final check." He turned to Jenny. "We know for sure this is what's been causing your trouble, but we may as well give it a three-month check. I'm not going to have you without a car for one minute longer so you take mine until tomorrow night."

Jenny started to refuse but Fletch handed her his keys. "Don't argue with me," he said. "I'll just drive yours to work in the morning. If it stops I know what to do."

"OK, if that's what you really want," Jenny said. She stuck her head into the Mustang. "Come on, Annie, your daddy's through working now."

Annie and Charley started to come out but before they stepped out, Jenny heard Annie whisper, "I love you too, Mommy."

Charley walked Annie to the old pickup and put her inside. Vince gathered up his tools and crawled in beside his little girl.

Fletch stood with Charley and Jenny. He stuck his hand through the window. "Thanks a million, Vince. I really appreciate your cooperation, as well as your skill."

"You solved the mystery," Vince said, shaking Fletch's hand. "Besides, I'm always glad to help." Vince's eyes met Charley's and melted to a soft sky blue. "Especially for Charley's roommate," he added.

Jenny got Fletch's Thunderbird started and headed up the hill before everything clicked in her mind.

That voice on the telephone! Vince! Of course, but what else was going on? "Hey, what's this 'Mommy' stuff?" she asked.

Charley batted her eyes. "Why nothin', ma'am," she said innocently. "The kid just needs a mother."

9

Jenny couldn't have been more pleased. "So Vince has been the guy all along?" she asked as she turned onto Northwest Twelfth.

"Vince and Annie," Charley said. "I love Annie as much as Vince." Her eyes twinkled. "In a different way, of course."

Jenny parked the car in the garage, and the girls walked up the sidewalk. After unlocking the kitchen door, Jenny pushed it open. They took off their coats and hung them up. "Annie loves you, too, Charley," Jenny said as they washed their hands to make supper. "How come I haven't noticed that at school?"

Charley chuckled. "We've been playing a game, Jen. We were seeing who could fool you the longest. Annie's a smart kid."

Jenny pulled out two cans of soup. "Soup OK, Charley?" she asked. "I'm beat." She waited for Charley's nod, opened the cans, and dumped the contents into a pan. "How come you kept it so secret? And why didn't he ever come to the house?" She poured in water and turned on the burner.

"Jen," Charley said severely, "do you remember when you introduced me to Vince? He didn't even see me. Why would I bring him around you when I knew he'd rather have you?"

"I'm sorry, Charley," Jenny said. "I'm sure you're wrong, but I'm sorry you feel that way."

A dreamy look passed over Charley's face. "Oh, I don't anymore. I'm sure of him now. Now that you know, he and Annie'll be around a lot. He really loves me, Jen. How could he love me so much?"

"How couldn't he, Charley?" Jenny asked. "You're pretty special."

Charley gently laid down her spoon. "Talkin' about special," she said, "did you notice Fletch didn't even ask what we were doin' at his place?" She nodded dreamily. "He's really special, Jen. Don't mess up with him."

Later, as she lay in bed, Jenny thought about Charley's remark. *What's to mess up?* she asked herself.

The next afternoon she returned Fletch's Thunderbird and marched down the long path to the service counter. Fletch's face brightened at the sight of her. "Your car is ready at last," he said, his dimples accenting his smile. "I had it washed and waxed as well as the mundane things like changing the oil, filter, and stuff like that. Just a touch of service to make up for all the trouble you've had."

Jenny felt her heart breaking into small pieces and washing away with the scrub water. She'd never see him again. She wouldn't be coming back and she knew he wouldn't call.

"Thanks for everything," she said, smiling. "And you never even asked what we were doing in front of your house. Charley tricked me. She took me to see the house before she told me who lived in it. I'm sure you know I felt like a world-class fool."

"Don't worry about it," he said. "People come to look at the house all the time. It's listed in *Pendleton's Guide to*

Historical Homes. You see, it was built in 1889. You should come see the inside sometime. Still all the original wood and some other things, too."

He walked Jenny to her car and helped her in. She drove away with tears in her eyes and a pain in her chest.

Bailey Miller visited Jenny each week and invited her to the Sabbath services. "I'd love to go, but right now, I'd rather not see someone who attends your church," she confessed.

Bailey laughed in his own happy contagious way. "I wouldn't worry about that if I were you. We have over 800 people attending each week and you aren't likely to see anyone you know. Is it really important that you not see this person? Perhaps if I knew who it is, I could help you avoid him or her. Or am I out of line asking?"

Jenny hesitated. But she'd developed a great trust in Bailey and knew her visits with him were confidential. She decided she could tell him. "It's Fletcher Leighton."

The minister failed to conceal his surprise. "Fletcher Leighton! Has he injured you in some way?"

Jenny shook her head. "No, he's a wonderful person and he's been especially kind to me. My reasons for avoiding him are entirely personal."

The minister sighed with relief. "I'm glad to hear that. Fletch isn't just another church member, you know. He's almost a minister and very active in all our programs, especially soul winning. Ordinarily he's the first person I'd introduce you to, for he has a special way with people, as well as a very unusual relationship with his Lord."

Jenny nodded. "I'm aware of all this, and I appreciate him a lot, but could you please just keep me out of his sight for a while?"

Bailey thought a moment, then smiled. "Sure, but when

you're baptized everyone will be watching and rejoicing, including Fletch."

"I know. I'll just have to figure out a way to stay out of his sight after that."

"You know, I usually discuss my Bible studies with Fletch, but we've both been so busy we just haven't gotten together for a while." The young minister glanced curiously at Jenny again. "Are you sure it's not something I can help you straighten out?"

Jenny flushed. "No, it isn't like that at all." She stopped, groping for words.

Bailey reached for her hand. "It's all right," he said. "I didn't mean to pry. Now, if you slip into the sanctuary just before services begin and leave a bit early, you'll never see him—or me either, for that matter."

Jenny did as the minister had advised. She slipped into one of the back rows each week and out before the closing hymn. She had made up her mind to forget Fletch and knew her heart would heal faster without the trauma of seeing him.

One evening Vince and Annie ate supper with Charley and Jenny. After supper Charley said, "We have something to tell you, Jen."

Jenny sat on the couch and gathered Annie to her side.

Charley crooked her finger at Annie and the girl climbed into her lap. Charley whispered something into Annie's ear. Annie laughed out loud and turned to Jenny. She opened her mouth but nothing came out. She took several deep breaths and jabbed a finger at Charley's chest. Her cheeks flushed a rosy pink. "She's really truly going to be my mommy now," she finally blurted.

Ugh! Jenny understood. Why didn't she think of this sooner?

"We're gettin' married a week from next Sunday, Jen,"

Charley said, almost softly, "and I want you to be my attendant. My maid of honor, I guess." She pulled Annie closer. "This little thing's goin' to be my flower girl."

Vince beamed his happiness and Jenny had to be glad for them all. But what would she do? She had grown to love her wild, crazy Charley very much.

They celebrated with root beer in plastic champagne glasses. Charley smiled into Vince's eyes. "Just to help you understand," she said with love-filled eyes, "we have class around here."

He hugged her close. "Just the kind of class I love," he said into her ear.

The next morning while Jenny listened to her best reading group she happened to think, *How am I going to pay the rent?* Shoving the horrible thought away, she continued listening to her pupils. As soon as the last child left the room Jenny rushed to Charley. "I can't pay the rent and electricity bill alone, Charley. What can I do?"

Charley's green eyes opened wide and wrinkles creased her forehead. "I'd forgotten all about that," she said after a moment. "I'd been thinking we roomed together because we were good friends."

Jenny's arms opened and Charley walked in. "We're best friends, my crazy Charley," Jenny whispered into the red brush. "I love you."

Charley pushed Jenny to arm's length. "But the problem still remains," she said with determination. "I guess we'll just have to find you a less pretentious place."

"Do you think we can?" Jenny asked. "I couldn't find any other apartments in the whole town. Of course, I didn't know the town, then. And I really fell in love with that one."

Charley bobbed her head up and down. "Sure. There have to be some." She smiled into Jenny's eyes. "You're so spoiled you may not like a cheapie, though."

The girls finished up the work and went home. Vince and Annie appeared for supper again. Afterward, as they ate chocolate chip cookies and drank milk, Charley brought up the subject again, and asked Vince if he knew of any nice but cheap apartments.

"I'm not sure, but I'll look into it." He rubbed his chin, thinking. "When you're ready, I can move you with the pickup," he added.

The next evening, after Charley had gone off with Vince and Annie, the phone rang. "Vince told me you need to find a cheaper place," Fletch's rich voice said into Jenny's ear. "I know of some apartments out near your school. I don't know how much they'd be, but they look cheaper."

Still catching her breath from the unexpected call, Jenny said, "Thanks, Fletch. Let me get a piece of paper and I'll take the address."

She got the paper then waited—and waited. "I have the paper now," she said softly.

"Well, I just wondered if you'd like for me to take you over. I'm free after supper tonight," he added quietly.

Her heart pounded against her ribs. Of course she would! But seeing him only increased the pain of realizing she couldn't have him. She finally managed to get some air into her lungs. "Thanks a lot," she stammered, "but I think I can find it." She tried to laugh but it came out weak. "After all," she continued, "I have to learn to be a big girl someday, and I know the town a little now."

He gave her the address, asked about her car, and hung up.

"Want to go look?" Jenny asked Charley the next morning at breakfast. "You might get a big laugh. You

106

know, your roommate going from riches to rags in one quick hop."

"I'll let you know, Jen," Charley said. "Maybe Vince and Annie would like to see it, too."

"Maybe you three would like to rent an apartment out there, too," Jenny suggested hopefully.

Charley filled the soap cups and turned on the dishwasher. She straightened up and looked at Jenny with surprise. "Jen, Vince has his own house and we've been fixing it up. You'll have to see it."

Remembering the decrepit old house, Jenny wasn't too eager, but of course she would see it, for Charley.

Vince and Annie arrived in the old pickup before Charley and Jenny finished supper. They left the dishes on the table and piled into the Mustang, everyone as excited as though headed for an evening of entertainment.

They went southwest through Pendleton and out Highway 395 to 30th Avenue, turned right, and back to 29th. "Hey Jen, it's on a hill, too," Charley yelled when she saw the faded yellow paint of the building. Jenny's first glance told her she couldn't live in it.

When she voiced her doubts Charley took over. "We have an appointment, Jen, so be quiet and look at it."

The owner of the house, a woman, led the group up a long flight of wooden stairs in the middle of the front of the building. A sidewalk-width deck at the top of the stairs led to the door of the vacant apartment.

The woman unlocked the door, threw it open, and stepped back. With Annie leading the way they all trooped in, Jenny entering last.

The apartment looked better inside than out, but it was so very plain and tiny compared to the one she lived in now. The vari-colored brown carpet in the living room was worn but clean. She eased to the kitchen door and peeked in. A couple of feet of cabinets, a tiny stove, and room for a small table.

"Whoa! This is cute," Charley said. Jenny flashed a look at her. She seemed sincere.

"Could we see the bedrooms, please?" she asked the woman.

The landlady led the way, opened a door, and Jenny saw the tiniest bathroom she'd ever seen. Shower, toilet, and sink in less space than her tub occupied at home. It looked clean, though.

"The bedroom is this way," the landlady said, walking down the short hall. Jenny wasn't surprised to find a closet-sized bedroom with dark purple carpet and freshly laundered lavender curtains.

"One bedroom, I guess," Jenny said. "How much?"

"It's a good solid building and clean as an operating room." The woman smiled proudly. She named a figure that was less than half what Jenny paid for her luxury apartment. "First and last months in advance."

"I'll take it," Jenny said, thinking that the electricity couldn't be much in a tiny place like that. "When may I move in?"

"Tonight," the lady said. "As soon as you pay the rent."

"But you better give notice where you are, don't you think?" Vince asked hesitantly. "I'm afraid you may end up paying rent on both places for a month." His face looked apologetic, as though he were intruding.

Jenny settled on giving the lady a retainer to hold the room and went home. She gave her notice that night and started packing, although she couldn't move yet. Charley packed too, with a vengeance. She would be moving in less than two weeks.

The day of Charley's wedding came all too soon and Jenny helped her dress in the small church she had chosen. "Hurry, Jen, are we late?" Charley asked for the third time.

Jenny continued carefully applying makeup to Charley's face. Jenny's rosy lips formed an "o" as she lightly applied the lipstick to Charley's generous mouth. "Relax. We have plenty of time. Just let me make you the most beautiful bride in the world."

Annie, wearing a white gown nearly like the bride's, peered at Charley. "She's already the prettiest bride in the world, Aunt Jenny, and the most gorgeousest mommy."

Jenny stooped and hugged Annie close. "You're right, Annie," she said. She released the little girl and picked up the curling iron. "Charley, would you like to leave Annie with me while you go on your honeymoon?" She rolled a small wisp of red hair as she talked.

Charley shook her head so violently Jenny lost the curl. "No way. This honeymoon's for the whole family," she said.

In a little while the wedding was over and the new family rattled away in the old pickup truck for their brief honeymoon in the Blue Mountains.

Jenny moped around the rest of the day, went to school the next day, and drooped around all evening. How would she ever get used to the silence? Charley made a person forget how quiet a place could be.

Jenny taught without an aide for three days, and though she had 24 noisy students, she'd never felt so alone. And she could barely stand the apartment in the evenings.

She read the Bible. In the last few weeks she'd read the Bible nearly through in addition to reading the Gospels many times. Each time she opened the Bible Jesus spoke to her heart. She felt His love, cheering and comforting her.

Her love for Him multiplied in response, and her

loneliness lessened. She knew now, without a doubt, who her unfailing Friend was, the Friend who would never leave her. She began to wonder if He had someone else in mind for her lifelong companion than Fletch. She prayed for strength to go on and healing for her aching heart. Ready to make a lifetime commitment to her Saviour, she wanted to unite with the Seventh-day Adventist church. But she wished desperately that she could attend church where she could relax, without the fear of running into Fletch.

One evening the apartment superintendent called and told her he had new tenants for her apartment so she could leave anytime.

Then Charley came back to school and they made arrangements to move Jenny the following Sunday. Vince felt they could do it in an afternoon. After all, Jenny didn't have that many things.

Jenny started packing in earnest and had nearly everything in boxes by Friday night. She spent a quiet Sabbath with her Saviour amidst the clutter. She smiled to herself as she realized that He was the only One she'd allow in her messy apartment.

Finally, Sunday afternoon came. Vince backed his old pickup to the kitchen door and started loading boxes. When he pulled away, another pickup backed up to the door and Fletch hopped out.

"Hope you don't mind," he said. "Vince happened to mention what he was doing this afternoon, so I decided to crash."

His dimples flashed and Jenny dropped into a chair by the kitchen table to catch her breath. How long would he be able to do this to her? She absolutely must get hold of herself.

He waited a moment, then asked, "Should I start taking the furniture now?"

Jenny nodded. "I'll help you carry the tables and chairs out."

They soon had the small furniture loaded as well as the few dishes and food she had left out. Fletch roamed through the apartment and stopped in front of the wall of windows. "I guess it's going to be tough getting used to a less fantastic place," he said, taking in the lovely view.

Jenny nodded. "I guess so," she said, "but the hardest part will be no Charley." She took a deep breath to push the threatening tears back. "It's amazing how she grew on me," she said, laughing quietly to hide the pain.

"Well, maybe you'll have a new roommate one of these days," he said, picking up a magazine rack and striding toward the kitchen door.

Jenny followed. "Not in that apartment," she said. "It has only one bedroom."

Vince and Charley returned and the men loaded the rest of the furniture into Fletch's black pickup.

Charley stayed and the girls gave the place a final cleaning. Then they drove Vince's old pickup to the new place.

Everyone helped Jenny get settled until about six o'clock, when Annie sidled up to Charley and pulled her head down. "I'm hungry, Mommy. Could you find some peanut butter?" she whispered into Charley's ear so loudly everyone heard.

"No way, angel," Charley bellowed. "I have supper ready at home." She stood up. "I mean for everyone." She took Annie's hand, put her arm around Vince's trim waist, and steered them toward the front door. "Come soon, you guys, we'll have it ready in half an hour."

Jenny shook her head. "I don't know, Cha—" she began.

Fletch interrupted. "We'll be along in a few minutes. As soon as we finish hanging this picture." He flashed his dimples at Jenny and her mouth went dry.

When they walked into Charley and Vince's living room, Jenny gasped. Freshly painted walls disappeared into soft new carpet. The kitchen had a fresh clean look, too. "Well, what do you think?" Charley asked at usual volume.

"Great. This house just needed a woman to make it shine," Jenny said.

"Well, a little more than that. But it's coming along. We have a bunch more planned, don't we, honey?" she asked Vince.

Annie tore into the kitchen and plopped herself at the table. She wiggled her fingers at Jenny. "Sit beside me, Aunt Jenny," she said eagerly. "Or do you have to sit by your boyfriend?"

Jenny's face grew warm, then hot. She couldn't open her mouth to say anything.

"Sure, pumpkin, she can sit by you," Fletch said, smiling at the little girl.

"Are you going to marry her like Daddy married my new mommy?" Annie asked Fletch, her eyes twinkling.

Jenny wished she could disappear. Fletch's face showed nothing. "I'm helping her get moved into her apartment," he said calmly. "Just like your daddy. That's what friends are for."

"Eat your dinner, Annie," Vince said quickly.

The meal progressed and after dessert Fletch stood up and looked at Jenny. "Think we should go get a little more done?" he asked, reaching for her coat.

Jenny settled into the pickup seat, wondering what she

could say. "Don't let Annie embarrass you," Fletch said, smiling kindly. "Everyone knows kids will say anything. Think we can get you put together so you'll be able to prepare for school tomorrow?"

"Oh, sure. I have the bed made and my clothes all put away. I just need to find enough dishes and food so I can eat breakfast."

"I could take you to breakfast."

"Not necessary," she assured him. "I know right where the things are. I'll be just fine."

Fletch washed the dishes for her "—since you don't have a dishwasher, anymore." Then he wiped down the cabinets and put the dishes away while she took care of the food.

Finally he put on his coat. "I may as well get out of your way, if I can't help anymore," he said.

Jenny stepped out onto the deck with him. "At least I can still see the city lights," she said.

He looked around. "You can, though not so close. But you're a lot closer to your school."

He started down the long outside stairway. She stood at the top looking down. "Thanks so much, Fletch," she said. "You're always there when I need you. How can I repay you?"

He bounded up beside her. "No thanks necessary, Jenny. Can't you tell I enjoy helping you?"

10

Fletch's words thrilled Jenny but somehow she knew he wouldn't call. And he didn't. Charley and Vince invited her for supper once or twice a week and she loved being "Aunt Jenny."

Martin Mandell invited her out several times and each time she refused as kindly as possible. But one morning his suggestion sounded too good to miss. "It's the last ballet of the season," he said, "and, I hear, the best."

Jenny smiled at him. "You know my vulnerable spots, don't you?" she asked. Why shouldn't she go with him? If anything was ever going to happen between her and Fletch it would have happened long before this. For sure, he didn't care a fig about her. "Sure, I'll go. I'd love to."

"Great. I'll pick you up at eight o'clock Friday night. We'll have dinner afterwards. Thanks a lot, Jenny. I've missed you."

Friday night! God's holy Sabbath day! Not hers, but His. After finally accepting Martin's invitation, she was really eager to go. But no way would she break her commitment to Him!

She shook her head. "I'm sorry, Martin, but I can't go on Friday night."

Martin gladly switched to Sunday night, and Jenny

enjoyed the beautiful music and graceful movements more than she imagined. Afterwards, at dinner, feeling guilty, she explained to Martin that they could only be friends. He didn't ask her out again.

As the weeks passed, her new Saviour, His church, and being the best teacher possible, became Jenny's entire life. Bailey Miller, the pastor, urged her to come to other meetings in addition to church services. He told her she would make new friends, men and women. She wished she could. And she would. But she couldn't handle the possibility of seeing Fletch right now while she so desperately tried to forget her feelings for him. As soon as her heart stopped hurting when she thought of him, she would join in many church activities.

One morning Leona Jones, the school secretary, ran into Jenny's classroom, interrupting her art class. Obviously excited, she signalled for Jenny to come. Jenny turned to Charley. "Could you take over, Mrs. Rogers?"

Charley raised her eyebrows. "You bet." Then she whispered, "Could you say 'Mrs. Rogers' again?"

Jenny stepped into the hall with Leona, who turned worried eyes on her. She put her hand on Jenny's arm. "There's a call for you," she said hesitantly. "You'd better come now."

The secretary's mannerisms set up a warning signal in Jenny's mind. "Who's calling?" she whispered, not wanting an answer.

The secretary didn't respond but walked quickly to the office and pointed at the phone. Jenny put the receiver to her ear. "This is Jennifer Cornell," she said.

"Miss Cornell," a crisp feminine voice said, "I'm Amelia Kirkwood, the admitting nurse at Grande Ronde Hospital in LaGrande."

Jenny looked behind her and sank into the leather chair against the wall.

"Your father has been in an accident," the voice continued smoothly. "Could you come to be with your mother?"

"Of course." Her own voice revealed nothing of her terror. "What happened?"

"It would be better for you to just come," the nurse said impersonally. "When may I tell your mother to expect you?"

Jenny looked around for her principal but he was nowhere to be seen. "I'll be there in two hours," she said. She hung up the phone with shaking hands. She knew it was bad. Otherwise Mom would have called. Or the nurse wouldn't have called. It was really bad.

Jenny stood on wobbly legs and hurried back to her room. "You'll be able to take over the class with no problem," Jenny told Charley with assurance. "At least I'll know my kids are in good hands."

"But you can't go alone under these circumstances," Charley said.

"I have to. And now." Jenny felt tears threatening so she hugged Charley and went in search of Mr. Brock.

The principal told her to go at once, but Charley intercepted Jenny before she got to the outside doors. "Fletch is on his way, Jen," she said, her eyes red around the edges. "I couldn't let you go alone. You could be the next accident."

Jenny hugged Charley again, unable to speak, and started toward the door. As she walked down the sidewalk, Fletch's brown Thunderbird roared up to the school and slid to a stop, the front end bouncing up and down.

The door opened and Fletch burst out, running toward the building. When they met he didn't speak but put his arm around her shoulder and steered her to his car. Taking off as fast as he'd arrived, Fletch drove through Pendleton and onto the freeway.

"Thanks again, friend," Jenny ventured after awhile. "But I could have driven, you know. My car works fine."

"You don't look too self-sufficient at the moment," he said with a small smile. "I'm glad Charley called." He drove in silence. "Charley's a real friend," he finally added.

Jenny nodded. Dear, loud, wild Charley certainly had become special.

Later Fletch looked caringly at Jenny. "Can you tell me what happened?"

She shook her head. "No," she whispered. "I don't know anything except that my dad's been in an accident and they wanted me to come."

He punched the accelerator a little more. "Sorry, Jenny," he said. "I'm sure he'll be all right though."

They didn't talk much. Fletch put his hand on the radio several times, but withdrew it without turning any knobs. Jenny, thankful she didn't have to listen to rock music, prayed silently to her newfound heavenly Father.

Finally, after an eternity, Fletch walked with her through the wide emergency room doors. As they followed a nurse to a waiting room, a strong smell of antiseptic nearly overwhelmed Jenny. Then her mother ran to meet them, her arms outspread. She sobbed into Jenny's neck for some time before she could speak. "They say he won't live," she cried.

Jenny held her again. How could they get along without Dad? Though a terrible tease, he was the solid rock in their lives. Fletch sat a little apart from the women, his elbows on his knees, his head resting in his hands, his eyes closed.

"What happened, Mom?" Jenny asked. "Was it a traffic accident?"

Mom nodded. "It happened on the way to work this morning. They tell me the man who hit Dad was dead drunk. Didn't even get a scratch." She broke down again and Jenny held her.

After leaving the women alone awhile, Fletch came and sat beside Jenny. "Could you girls eat a bowl of soup?" he asked. "You may have a long vigil, so you should keep up your strength."

Mom shook her head and Jenny didn't feel hungry either. "Thanks anyway, Fletch," she said. "Why don't you go on back? I can come on the bus or something. I may be here all day—even all night."

"No, I'm going to wait with you," he said with a tight smile. "Do you know what's going on right now?" he asked Mrs. Cornell.

"They haven't told me much," she said, sobbing quietly.

Jenny stood up. "I'm going to see what I can find out." She marched to the nurse's desk.

The nurse looked at some papers on the desk, than back at Jenny. "I'll try to get a doctor," she said quietly. She picked up the phone and Jenny went back to Mom and Fletch.

In a few minutes a small middle-aged man dressed in hospital green approached the group. "I'm Dr. Hague," he said, shaking Fletch's hand. "We're still running tests on Mr. Cornell, but I have to tell you it doesn't look good. Both legs and his pelvis are broken as well as undetermined internal injuries. He's also in deep shock." He hesitated a moment, then continued. "It should have been the other man. Nothing makes me so angry as accidents caused by drunks."

"Are they operating, Dr. Hague?" Fletch asked.

The doctor looked into Fletch's eyes and slowly shook his head. "No, son, they're trying to determine the extent of his injuries. And he's in no condition to handle surgery right now." He turned away, took several brisk steps, and turned back. "I'll be back as soon as I know anything." He disappeared through the double doors.

Fletch excused himself and walked off down the hall. Jenny silently prayed for her father. Mrs. Cornell stared at a picture on the opposite wall, but Jenny knew she didn't see it. In a little while Fletch returned with two paper cups of potato soup. "Here," he said firmly, "I want you both to eat this, even if you don't want it." He handed each woman a cup and plastic spoon.

"Eat your soup, Jenny," he said a little later. "It's getting cold. You too, Mrs. Cornell." They both took a bite. Then another.

An hour passed and Fletch disappeared again. This time he brought hot chocolate and made them drink it.

Then he brought two pillows from somewhere and told Jenny and her mother to try to sleep for a little while. After resisting, Mrs. Cornell dropped into a fitful sleep for nearly an hour.

"Fletch, you're an angel in disguise," Jenny said. "Where did you ever learn to be so thoughtful?"

Fletch shrugged, chuckling softly. "Just doing what needs to be done," he replied.

Jenny smiled too, remembering the time she'd used the same words to Fletch in reference to helping the man in the pickup wreck.

Later Fletch brought trays of light supper and coaxed the women to eat most of it. They still had no word from Dr. Hague. *How long can this go on?* Jenny wondered. In a little while they would all be ready for padded rooms.

Fletch brought something to drink every hour or so. "Fletch," Mrs. Cornell said, after he brought tall paper cups filled with iced orange juice, "I've never seen anyone so kind. No matter how this turns out, you've made it a little more bearable. How can we ever repay you?"

He leaned close to her. "What I long to do, Mrs. Cornell, is to pray with you. Our heavenly Father is waiting to help. I know He is."

Mrs. Cornell didn't hesitate an instant. "Of course. Where?"

Fletch looked around. "Right here." He pulled his chair around in front of Jenny and Mrs. Cornell. Then he put his arms around both of them as they remained sitting, and drew them into a close circle, the tops of the three heads nearly touching as they bowed.

Then he prayed an eloquent prayer for Mr. Cornell's healing. He also prayed for them all to know and love Him. When Fletch finished all three faces were tear-stained. But something had touched them and Jenny marveled at Fletch's faith. How close he must be to his Lord. She felt very close, too, but she'd never dared to pray as he had.

They all leaned back and rested. Sometime after midnight, Jenny felt someone shaking her. "Miss Cornell." Jenny jumped to her feet when she saw Dr. Hague. Was Dad gone? But the doctor was smiling and Mom and Fletch were on their feet too, eagerly listening.

"About eleven o'clock something happened," the doctor said. "Mr. Cornell regained consciousness and his vital signs stabilized. He's in surgery, now. We think he's going to make it." The doctor shook his head in wonder. "You just never know about people," he said. "Maybe that's what makes the practice of medicine so satisfying."

Mrs. Cornell put her hand on the doctor's arm. "But we know what happened," she said. "This young man called on his God to heal my husband at that exact time."

The doctor shook hands with Fletch. "Around here, we never take prayers lightly, son," he said. "We appreciate all the help we can get. I suppose you folks will want to stay until he comes out of surgery."

"Of course," Fletch said. "We wouldn't be any other place."

After the doctor had gone, Mom said, "Fletch, you better thank your God for what He just did. I'm so excited I can hardly contain myself. We've just seen a miracle."

Jenny, who had been wondering how to tell her mother that she was joining this "strange" church, decided this must be the perfect time. She took her mother's hand. "Mom," she said, "I've been wanting to tell you something but didn't know how you'd feel about it. Fletch goes to the Seventh-day Adventist church, and I'm going to join that church in two weeks—if Daddy's all right."

Fletch came off his chair as though it were electrified. "What did you say?" he shouted. Jenny had heard Fletch shout only once. When he fixed her car. Her mouth dropped open and she gazed at him in astonishment.

He couldn't stand still. He jerked her to her feet and engulfed her in a hug that nearly mashed her. A moment later he pushed her to arm's length. "What did you just say to your mother?" he thundered again.

"I said I'm joining your church," Jenny repeated. "Bailey said you have a way with people, but do you act like this every time you have a convert?"

Fletch dropped his arms. He looked at Jenny, then at her mother. His face flushed a rosy red and he smiled wryly. Then he shook his head. "No, I guess I don't." He glanced at Mrs. Cornell. "I'm sorry," he said. "Let's sit down."

After they returned to their chairs he reached for Jenny's hand and held it gently in his two much larger ones. After a moment he smiled—and Jenny caught her breath. He leaned to her ear. "I acted that way because I

121

like you a lot," he whispered.

Jenny could hardly believe her ears! And why did he choose this particular time to tell her? She felt tears behind her eyes again, but that was all right. Everyone would think it was because of Dad.

Jenny peeked at Fletch through her tears and their eyes met. She mouthed one word. "Why?"

"Why?" His brown eyes opened wide. "Why do I like you? Because you're so nice—and caring—and kind."

"Why did you tell that guy I wasn't for you?"

His eyes opened wide in surprise, but then he smiled broadly, his dimples making her already errant heart dance more wildly. "You heard that?" He looked off into space a moment, then shrugged. "You had just told me rather strongly that you didn't like Christian music. If you couldn't even handle Christian music, I figured you must be really anti-religious."

Jenny began laughing, tears running down her cheeks. "I didn't say that," she said. "I said I didn't like rock. I hate rock. I thought your concert was gospel rock. I love most music, including religious music."

A doctor approached, his heels thumping on the white tile floor. "The Cornells?" he asked. Everyone jumped up.

"I'm Dr. Gregg." The tall white-haired man extended his hand to Fletch. "We just put Mr. Cornell back together and he seems pretty good. Considerably better than we first believed. And his internal injuries were much less serious than we thought. All in all, he's doing extremely well."

Jenny looked at Fletch and smiled, but Mom told the doctor all about Fletch's prayer. The doctor nodded. "I suspected some help from the Man upstairs," he said. "He steps in quite often. Now, Mr. Cornell won't awaken until morning. Why don't you folks go home for a few hours?"

The doctor walked away, looking tired but happy.

Jenny drove Mom's car home and Fletch followed. Inside the house, Mom slumped onto the couch. "Why do I feel as though I had been in the accident?" she asked. Without waiting for an answer she looked from Jenny to Fletch, and back to Jenny. "I'm pleased you're joining a church, Jenny," she said, "but what happened after you told me?"

Jenny laughed and scooted closer to her mother. "I'm not sure, Mom. Fletch seemed pretty happy to learn I'm joining his church."

"I am happy," Fletch said. "But you girls are so very tired. It's time to go to bed. We can talk about it tomorrow."

"Would you do something for me first?" Mrs. Cornell asked.

"Of course. Name it."

"Pray for Dad once more. Would you please?"

Snuggling in her bed later, Jenny thought about Fletch's prayers for her father. She knew—she just knew—Dad would be all right. Fletch had prayed so sincerely and with such faith. She remembered many places in the New Testament that say if we ask in faith He hears and answers our prayers.

Then she thought about Fletch telling her that he liked her a lot. It almost seemed as if an invisible wall had fallen from between them at that moment. She had always unconsciously felt that barrier, but what had it been? And why had it disappeared when Fletch learned she was joining his church? Finally she fell asleep and slept soundly until the fragrance of coffee brewing brought her wide awake.

"Have you talked to the hospital this morning?" she asked her mother as she walked into the cheery kitchen and planted a kiss on the older woman's cheek.

Mom looked like a new person. "Yes, and he's doing fine. He's really going to be all right." She turned to Fletch, already seated at the table. "But we knew that last night, didn't we?" she asked.

He nodded. "Our Lord can do anything, Mrs. Cornell."

Jenny quietly made hot chocolate and served it to Fletch and herself and they enjoyed a relaxed breakfast before going to the hospital.

Two days later the little group walked into the hospital and down the now familiar hall to Dad's hospital room. Dad's eyes lit up in his pale face. "Well, if it isn't the auto mechanic, still keeping my little girl's motor running," he teased.

Fletch grasped Mr. Cornell's hand. "You look better every time we come," he said.

"I'm feeling great," the older man said, eyeing the contraption that held both legs high and in traction. "If you'll just get that thing off me, I'm ready to go home."

Mrs. Cornell laughed with delight. "I'm ready to take you home, too, love, but according to the doctors you're going to call this place home for some time. Maybe I'll just move in with you and we'll both be at home right here."

That evening at the Cornell home the three sat in the living room, talking. Fletch kept reaching for Jenny's hand, then releasing it. "I'm sorry, I can't help it," he whispered into her ear. "I just can't believe it."

Jenny straightened herself. "If you like me so much why didn't you call? Or come to see me? Or anything?"

He nodded vigorously. "I've been attracted to you from the moment our eyes met, but I knew we'd never make it if we didn't believe the same. I would have tried to teach you about our Lord Jesus, but when you refused to even listen to His music I thought it was hopeless."

"But I didn't refuse to listen to His music," Jenny reminded him. "I refused to listen to rock." He held her hand so tightly that she felt his heart beating.

He retrieved his hand and tapped her on the tip of her nose. "But I *thought* you were strongly irreligious," he explained. "It was the hardest battle I've ever had. In my mind I didn't want to get involved with you, but you were like a drug I couldn't live without. You were so good and sweet and kind. I kept thinking of reasons I had to see you, then realized I couldn't. Did you know the Bible says we shouldn't be unequally yoked? But how did you get interested in our church?"

She smiled, remembering. "Charley brought home some leaflets. I became interested and called Bailey Miller. I bought a Bible to learn about the Sabbath and ended up falling in love with my Saviour. I've been attending church, but sneaking out early so I wouldn't have to face you. I tried to get over you, Fletch, but it wouldn't stop hurting."

"I tried, too," Fletch said, "but it only got worse. I prayed about it until I gave up, thinking it could never be. And all the time our Lord was working it out for us to get to know each other better."

The next morning Fletch told Jenny that he must go back to Pendleton. "I can't let Dad discover he doesn't need me any more," he said at the breakfast table. "I need an excuse to stay here for a while, since I'd like to delay my return to Andrews until next fall."

Jenny drained her milk glass and wiped her mouth with a linen napkin. "Could you stay another day?" she asked. I really should see Dad once more, then I'd go back with you. Charley's probably going out of her head, trying to handle my third graders alone."

Fletch thought a moment, then nodded his head. "Sure, why not?" He winked. "I'd be glad for the company on the ride back. And I want to see you a lot from now on. You won't need to hide from me at church, anymore. In fact I'll take you to church—and all the other meetings. After I introduce you to all the young people at church I guarantee you'll never be lonely again."

"And I want to be the one to tell Charley the news."

Mom walked into the room, her hair damp from the shower. "What news is this, dear?" she asked Jenny.

For some reason Jenny felt shy. "Well, just—well, Charley once told me that Fletch and I walked to the beat of different drummers, didn't speak the same language, and didn't even sing the same song."

Fletch interrupted with a happy wink for Mrs. Cornell. "We're both eager for her to know we're definitely marching to the same Drummer. Possibly we speak the same language. And who knows, we may even sing the same song."